"It **dea for us**
to be alone,

Jed said, looking at her lips.

Abby shook her head. "A terrible idea."

Jed took a step closer. "We're old enough to know better."

"Definitely old enough," she agreed.

Jed removed his hat and dropped it on the ground. Then he brushed his lips against hers in a teasing caress. "As long as we keep both feet on the ground we should be safe."

"Hmm" was all she could manage. The man knew how to kiss, was the one and only thought Abby managed before her brains evaporated into the bright Wyoming sunshine. His lips were firm and warm, coaxing hers to part. Abby clung to him, fingers hooked in his leather belt, while his tongue did lovely things to her mouth and his large, work-roughened hands slipped under her T-shirt.

"Jed," she whispered, pulling away from his mouth a fraction of an inch. "We can't do this."

He loosened his hold on her.

"You said we'd be okay if we stayed on our feet," she said, trying to tease away the tension between them.

"I was wrong. We could do it standing up without much trouble." He picked up his hat and dusted it off before putting it back on his head. "But you're safe now. A cowboy never makes love with his hat on."

A busy mother of six and married for over twenty-five years, **Kristine Rolofson** writes about family life in many of her books. A finalist in Romance Writers of America's Golden Heart contest in 1986, Kristine's first book sold shortly afterward to Harlequin Temptation. At first she combined writing with such jobs as waitress, wallpaper hanger, secretary and seamstress. Now she writes full-time and is the author of over twenty novels.

Kristine confesses to having no hobbies, unless keeping up with the laundry is considered an extracurricular activity.

Don't miss the next BOOTS & BOOTIES book in December 1998, #712 *The Right Man in Montana*.

Books by Kristine Rolofson

HARLEQUIN TEMPTATION
507—PLAIN JANE'S MAN
548—JESSIE'S LAWMAN
560—MAKE-BELIEVE HONEYMOON
569—THE COWBOY
617—THE LAST MAN IN MONTANA (Boots & Booties)
621—THE ONLY MAN IN WYOMING (Boots & Booties)
625—THE NEXT MAN IN TEXAS (Boots & Booties)

Kristine Rolofson
THE WRONG MAN IN WYOMING

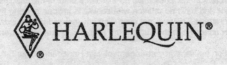

TORONTO • NEW YORK • LONDON
AMSTERDAM • PARIS • SYDNEY • HAMBURG
STOCKHOLM • ATHENS • TOKYO • MILAN • MADRID
PRAGUE • WARSAW • BUDAPEST • AUCKLAND

For Ben, Will and Tony,
the three Rolofson boys
who make their mother proud.

ISBN 0-373-25792-9

THE WRONG MAN IN WYOMING

Copyright © 1998 by Kristine Rolofson.

Printed in U.S.A.

1

"WHEN ARE WE gonna get there?"

Abby figured that could easily be the four-thousandth time she'd heard the same question. She eased her grip on the steering wheel and took a deep breath before answering her son once again.

"Three more days till we reach Grandma's house," she managed, as another enormous truck screamed past them on the interstate.

"I'm not talkin' about Grandma's house," the child moaned. "I mean the motel. When are we gonna get there so we can go swimming?"

"Swimming!" Cass screeched from her car seat in the back of the minivan. "I wanna go swimming."

Abby glanced in the rearview mirror to see her chubby five-year-old grinning at her. "And you will, honey. Pretty soon. After everyone has a rest."

"You said we could swim this afternoon," Matt reminded her. At eight he often acted at least thirty years old.

"I meant *late* this afternoon. We ate lunch twenty minutes ago. We have to go another two hundred miles or so today or we'll never get to Grandma's house. Why don't you take a nap?"

He opened his *Star Wars* book. "Naps are for babies."

"I'm not a baby," Cass insisted, her voice loud enough to wake every sleeping baby in Wyoming. "Chrissie's the baby."

And Chrissie could sleep through anything, thank goodness. Abby hoped the toddler would sleep, slumped to one side in her car seat, another hour or two. The afternoons were the most difficult times of the day, when the kids were tired of being cooped up in the van, when Abby's shoulders ached from driving and the glare of the sun hurt her eyes. She'd lost her sunglasses somewhere in Nebraska.

"No one said you were a baby," Abby told her. "Look out the window. Maybe you'll see a cow. Or a windmill."

Cows and windmills had begun to be the only things that broke up the monotony of the desolate Wyoming landscape. Acres of land stretched out on either side of the interstate, broken only by highway exits to towns called "Wheatland" and "Glenrock." A map of the western states lay folded on the floor in between the front seats, but part of Wyoming was stained with ketchup that Matt had dropped during lunch, leaving Abby unsure how many more miles of the state were left to cross. Washington and Grandma seemed very far away.

"Let's all have a quiet time now," she said, using her most official mother voice. "You can read or color or play with your toys, but let's be quiet so I can concentrate on driving."

"Can we wave to the trucks?" Matt asked hopefully. Some of the drivers honked when the children waved at them.

"Not until Chrissie wakes up."

The boy sighed. "I guess I'll read."

"Good idea." She glanced at Cass, whose blue eyes looked heavy. She'd doze off in no time as long as there wasn't a conversation to contribute to.

Abby couldn't wait for this day to be over. With any luck, they would be settled in a room at a Super 8 by four o'clock, ordering pizza by five and sleeping by eight o'clock. The van shook as another truck passed them. Wyoming, Abby thought, was hell.

"NO WAY IN HELL," Jed declared, tossing a saddle on his favorite mare. "You're too young."

"You're wrong, Uncle Jed," the young man said, standing his ground and thrusting out his chin. "I'm a grown man now. I've been out of school for a year, doing a man's work here."

Jed glanced at his nephew and held his temper in check. "You're a man, all right, Ty. A *young* man. A man who isn't thinking with his brain."

"There's nothing wrong with my brain."

"No, except that you're not using it. You don't want to get hooked up with a Jensen. They're nothing but trouble." He checked the cinch and gave the mare a pat on the neck. "That little gal has you in knots, son. You'd better get control of yourself. You're too young to settle down, too young to know what you want—and who you want—for the rest of your life. Take your time."

"You don't give me enough credit. Or Trish."

Jed turned and studied his nephew. He was tall and lean, with the same dark hair and dark eyes that characterized generations of Monroe men. He was stubborn, too, with the easy smile and slow temper he'd inherited from his father. "You know nothing about women."

"And you do?" the kid challenged. "How?"

"That's none of your business." Jed turned back to his horse and hoped Ty would have the sense to return to work. "You have work to do, so you might as well get at it. There's fence to check in the southeast pasture and someone needs to make sure the irrigation is working over there."

He heard the boy sigh. "You want me to do that now?"

"Yes."

"Fine."

"You home for supper?"

"I guess."

Jed swung himself into the saddle and watched Ty walk across the yard toward the house. The damn kid was going to get himself in trouble. Trish and Ty had managed to be together since they were young kids, even though God knew there was no love between the two families. Besides, nineteen was too damn young to know anything about love, but he couldn't tell Ty anything. The kid thought he knew it all.

Jed frowned as he watched the young man get into his truck. Ty was riding for a fall, all right, and Jed would do anything he could do to save the boy from a broken heart.

Jed turned away and rode toward the east pasture. It sure didn't look like this was going to be an easy summer.

"WHAT'S THAT SMELL?" Matt crinkled up his nose and fiddled with the air-conditioning lever.

"That doesn't work, honey. Open your window a little more."

"It stinks in here."

Abby leaned toward the vent. Sure enough, an odd smell radiated from underneath the dashboard. She checked in the rearview mirror before pulling over to the side of the gravel road, switched off the engine and pulled the lever to release the hood. Was that smoke billowing out?

She told herself it was only dust. She couldn't be having car trouble miles from anywhere. She'd taken the last exit off the interstate looking for bathrooms and ice cream cones. She'd taken a wrong turn returning to the highway, obviously, because the four-lane road was nowhere in sight. Just an empty road lined with sagebrush and dirt. And wind. Wind that blew dirt into her mouth and made her eyes water whenever she got out of the van. The relentless June sun showed no mercy as Abby opened her car door and stepped onto the empty road.

"What's the matter, Mommy?" Cass asked. "Where are you going?"

"To check the engine." Which was an optimistic statement. She could stare underneath the hood all afternoon and not know if something was right or wrong. She knew enough to know that smoke was not a good sign. She knew enough not to lift the hood and risk burning herself. Something was broken.

She straightened and pushed her hair off her face. Of course something was broken. Nothing had gone right in the past nineteen months. Why should this month be any different?

Matt stuck his blond head out of the car window. "Are we still going to Grandma's?"

"Sure," she said, putting her hands on her hips. It could be worse, she reminded herself. It could be a car accident. Or a sick child.

"Where are we?"

"Good question. Get the map, will you?" She figured her life was the domino theory of disaster. One led to another, one crisis tipping over another. And on and on, gathering momentum until it played itself out with the big finish, like when the domino experts showed off on talk shows. Dominos went uphill and down, triggering "oohs" and "aahs" from the audience until the last domino had collapsed on the stage.

"You better watch out for snakes." Matt dangled the map out of the window.

Abby looked around and walked gingerly to the passenger side of the van. "Snakes?"

"Yeah. We're out west, you know."

She squinted at the map. "I figured that out."

He squinted at her, his blond bangs dipping across his eyebrows. "Are we lost, Mom?"

Abby scraped a piece of dried ketchup off the map and peered at the names of the towns that lined the interstate. "Not exactly. But I think we have a problem with the van."

"What does that mean?"

"I don't know. But I don't think smoke is a good sign, do you?"

"We hafta call a tow truck," her son suggested.

"We should," Abby agreed. *Except your father kept the car phone.* She shaded her eyes and looked down the desolate stretch of road. "And we will. When we can find a house or a store that has a phone."

"Okay." Matt broke into song, the *Star Wars* theme, and held his plastic action figure out of the open window.

She returned to the front of the van and debated opening the hood. No, she'd heard too many stories of people being burned that way. Abby backed up a foot and considered her situation. She could take a chance and drive the van back the way they'd come. It couldn't be that far. Enough time to eat an ice cream cone, admire three or four cows, settle an argument about who sat in the front seat, and gradually realize there were no signs pointing the way to the main highway.

On the other hand, she didn't want to destroy her only means of transportation. She'd heard stories of that happening, too.

"Mommy!" Cass hollered. "Chrissie wants you!"

Sure enough, the sounds of her youngest's delicate whimpers could be heard over Matt's battle song. "I'm coming."

She took one more look at the van, smoke wafting from underneath the hood, and said a prayer that this would be a simple problem. A quick and inexpensive solution seemed too much to hope for, but she hoped for the best anyway. Abby climbed into the back of the van and comforted her youngest child until the baby smiled. Abby held the child on her lap and, hoping to see a car or two on the road, looked out the window. This was one of those times when she wished there was a man around to help out.

Fortunately she didn't feel that way very often.

"WE SHOULDN'T WAIT much longer."

"I know." Ty held her in his arms as they stood together beside the truck. "I'll figure out how to handle Uncle Jed." Surely he couldn't stay stubborn about this. Ty knew he and Trish were meant to be together.

Her arms tightened around his waist. "He needs kids of his own. Or at least a wife," Trish said. "Then he'd understand how we feel. And he'd be too busy to worry about you."

"I don't think he's real interested in getting married. He always says he's too busy and too old to start dating anybody." Though lots of women sure had tried to interest his uncle in more than a few casual dates, Ty knew. His uncle was a good-looking man. For his age.

Trish lifted those blue eyes and planted a kiss on Ty's chin. "Maybe that's because he hasn't met the right woman. Maybe he got his heart broken a long time ago and he never got over it."

Ty tried to picture Uncle Jed in love. He couldn't. "I don't know, Trish. He's never said anything about getting dumped."

"He probably wouldn't tell anyone. He's kind of quiet."

"He's just real busy," Ty said, thinking about how hard his uncle worked. "You know what ranching is like."

Trish stood on her tiptoes and brushed her lips against his. "I don't want to talk about ranching right now."

"I'm supposed to be checking fence." God, Trish was beautiful. All that long wavy hair. The color of butterscotch, Ty decided as he smoothed his fingers down its curly length. His heart ached from loving her so much.

"Right away?"

Ty grinned down at her. "I guess it can wait." They stopped talking for a while, until Ty knew that he'd better start checking fence line instead of kissing Trish. He didn't want a lecture during supper tonight. He planned to talk about getting married again and he wanted his uncle to be in a good mood when he brought up the subject.

"I'll call you tonight after I talk to Jed," he promised her before he drove away from the Jensen ranch.

"Okay. Dad isn't going to be home till late tonight."

Mr. Jensen was another problem, and Ty didn't look forward to dealing with that man. Half the time he was drunk, and the other half he was struggling to make his cattle business turn a profit.

Ty took the county road and had covered ten of the fifteen miles that separated the two ranches when he spotted the red van and the woman holding a baby. Ty slowed down and then, when he saw the Michigan license plate, pulled his truck to a stop.

"Ma'am? Are you in some kind of trouble?" he asked through the open window.

The relieved expression on her face told Ty he'd asked the right question. She was a pretty lady, with a real pretty little kid on her hip.

"Hi. I think my van overheated. Is there a town near here where I could take it to a gas station?"

"There's a real small town about fifty miles from here, but you might not want to drive that far with a hot engine." He turned off his engine and pulled the truck off to the side of the road. "Want me to take a look at it?"

"If you don't think it's too dangerous to lift the hood, that would be wonderful."

Ty grabbed his work gloves and readjusted his Stetson before hopping out of the truck and following the woman to the front of her minivan. Two kids leaned out of the windows and stared at him. It didn't take long to figure out that the lady had a radiator problem. He took a jug of water from the back of the truck and poured some into the radiator. He and the woman watched as it ran out underneath the van.

"This doesn't look good, ma'am." He left the hood open.

"I guess we're stranded," she said, leaning against the van. She sure looked nervous. "Can you call someone for us? Would you mind?"

"No trouble," Ty reassured her. "Where are you going?"

"We're moving to Washington. We stopped a little while ago to get gas and ice cream, and then I got a little lost."

"That was Billy's, about twenty miles back. Would have been quite a walk in this heat, and he doesn't do repair work." He stuck out his hand. "Name's Ty Monroe. I live near here."

"Abby Andrews," she said, shaking his hand. "Thanks for your help."

It was then that Ty felt the first flash of brilliance pierce his brain. Ty noticed the lady didn't wear a wedding ring. She also had a good figure and was polite, too. Her kids seemed nice enough, though the baby kept staring at him as if

she'd never seen a man before. Trish figured his
uncle acted cranky sometimes because he didn't
have a woman in his life. Made sense. Ty had
been a heck of a lot happier since he and Trish
had been together. Woke up smiling each morning, wondering when he would see her. Wondering if they'd be able to sneak off and be together
alone.

And here was a woman for Jed. A mature
woman. A pretty woman. A woman to occupy
Uncle Jed and keep him cheerful while Ty and
Trish made their wedding plans. Heck, it was
worth a try. Besides, he couldn't leave her here on
the county road.

"How about if you come back to the ranch with
me? Meanwhile one of my men can take a look at
your radiator and see what it needs."

"How far away is it?"

"Ten miles, more or less."

"Can I drive the van that far?"

He shook his head. "I wouldn't risk it, not with
a hot engine like that. I can put some of your
things in the back of the truck, then you and the
kids can ride up front with me. Might be a tight
fit, but we're not going far."

"I really appreciate the help, but—"

"Ma'am—"

"Abby," she corrected.

"Abby," Ty repeated. "I sure can't leave you
sitting in the road like this. Just wouldn't be
right."

"Are you sure your uncle won't mind?"

Ty grinned. "My uncle likes company, ma'am. I'm sure he won't mind a bit."

HE MINDED A LOT. Abby could tell that right away. Oh, the tall rancher tipped his hat to her, but he didn't smile. Not really. Those lips of his didn't turn upward, not a bit. He was a tall man, around forty, with a rangy body encased in dusty boots, denim jeans and a faded plaid work shirt. An old Stetson covered up most of his head, though Abby guessed his hair was as dark as his nephew's. They had the same brown eyes, the same high cheekbones and long noses. Handsome men, though the younger hadn't grown into his strong features quite yet. Ty's uncle climbed off a stocky black horse and gave the reins to the older man who waited for him.

"Thanks, Toby," he said, and the man nodded and led the horse away toward a cluster of barns and sheds. They stood in the shade of a porch that lined part of the sprawling two-story house. A couple of worn benches sat out of the sun, underneath sets of windows that faced the back pastures. It looked like an enormous place, but Abby didn't know much about ranches. But she did remember her manners.

"I'm Abby Andrews," she said, holding out her hand for him to shake. He removed his leather gloves and took her hand in a very brief but gentle grip.

"Jed Monroe." The man's expression seemed baffled as he looked down at her. Those dark eyes examined her briefly, glanced at the baby on her hip, the child who clung to her leg and the boy who stood next to Ty. The man then focused on his nephew. "I thought you were fixing fence."

"I had an errand." There was no apology in that answer.

The dark eyebrows rose as if he knew exactly where the young man had been and he didn't approve. His lips tightened and a muscle in his jaw clenched. Abby wished once again that her van had managed to hold together until it reached Spokane.

"Abby's from Michigan," Ty said. "She and her kids are moving to Washington this summer."

"Is that so." He didn't appear to be very interested in that news, and Abby didn't blame him. The man looked as if all he wanted was a hot shower and a good meal, not the intimate details of a stranger's itinerary.

Matt stared at the tall man and held out his hand. "I'm Matt. Are you a cowboy?"

The man may have smiled as he shook hands with her son, but Abby couldn't be sure. "I'm a rancher, son."

"Oh."

"Rancher," Cass repeated, testing the word. She pulled on Abby's arm. "Are we going swimming now?"

"No, honey. Not yet." She turned back to Mr. Monroe. "I'm really sorry to be such a nuisance," Abby said, wincing when Chrissie tugged on her hair.

Those dark eyes held hers for a long second. "It's no trouble. We'll see what we can do to help you on your way."

"Thank you."

Ty spoke. "I thought I'd ask Bull to take a look at it when he gets done with the calves. It's a red van, out on the county road about ten miles east of here."

"Between here and the Jensen place, I suppose."

The young man's chin lifted. "That's right." There was a moment of silence before he continued. "I think the radiator's causing all the trouble," Ty said. "Or maybe Abby's lucky and it just needs a new hose."

"I hope you're right," she told the young man. "I really need that van to hold up until we get to Spokane."

Jed Monroe removed his hat and slapped it across his thighs to remove the dust. "You're welcome to go inside the house and make yourself comfortable, Mrs. Andrews."

"Thank you," she said, "but we'll just wait out here on the porch for now."

He shrugged. "Suit yourself." He turned to his nephew. "Take over with the calves so Bull can look at that van. When you're done, check that fence line."

"Yes, sir."

Mr. Monroe turned to Abby and tipped his hat. "Ma'am," he murmured before he walked away.

Abby led the children to the benches and sat

with Chrissie on her lap. She watched Ty's uncle follow him to the barn. Obviously Ty hadn't done his work this afternoon, but Abby was glad the young man had helped them. Well, they would sit here by the house and try not to be any more trouble to these nice people. The men had work to do and the least she could do would be to stay out of their way.

Matt swung his legs and swatted at a fly. "Are we gonna go to a motel now?"

"In a little while." Abby readjusted Chrissie's weight so the baby could snuggle against her neck.

"Soon?" Cass asked.

"I sure hope so, honey." The sooner the Andrews were on their way, the better. Abby prayed that whatever was wrong with the van was simple and inexpensive to repair. She didn't know what she would do otherwise, but she refused to worry about that until she heard bad news. One crisis at a time was about all she could handle. And this hadn't qualified as a crisis.

At least not yet.

2

"I'LL GET to the fence later," Ty promised, meeting Jed at the door of the barn.

Jed nodded. "Soon, Ty."

"I couldn't leave that woman alone like that."

"No."

"She seemed real nice." Ty grinned. "Pretty, too."

Yes, Abby Andrews was a good-looking woman, if you liked the delicate, maternal type. She'd also seemed tired, but Jed figured anyone crazy enough to cross the country alone with three little children should know better. "Yeah. Now, what about—"

"She has cute kids, too."

Jed came close to losing his patience. Ty was trying his darnedest to find out if Jed was angry with him for going over to the Jensen place when he should have been working. Well, he wasn't going to pretend he was jumping for joy about it. "Do you mind if we talk business now?"

"I thought I'd go with Bull when he looks at the van."

"You've got other work to do," Jed reminded him. "I think he can find it himself."

"He might need help."

"He'll manage," Jed said.

"Maybe I'd better stay here, then, and help look after those kids. Abby looks like she could use an extra hand."

Jed couldn't hide his surprise. "You're offering to baby-sit?"

Ty managed to look sincere. "Well, we don't want anybody getting hurt around here. Last thing we need is a lawsuit."

"You'll be checking fence by flashlight."

The boy grinned. "Wouldn't be the first time."

Jed turned and watched Ty head back to the house. He was a good kid, ready to help a stranger or a friend. He was smart, too, graduated in the top third of his high school class, but had turned down the chance to go to college. Jed knew why and was helpless to prevent the boy from making a big mistake.

Could he stop him from making another? A man shouldn't rush into marriage, especially when he was only nineteen. Not at any age, come to think of it. But he hadn't figured out a way to make Ty slow down and listen to reason.

He'd solve one problem at a time, and right now he needed to check on those calves. Ty could take care of Abby Andrews and her little family while Bull checked the van. In an hour or two, they'd be on their way to wherever they were going and he would have one less thing to worry about.

TY FIGURED he was really smart this time. For a

nineteen-year-old he wasn't doing too bad, he told himself as he dialed Trish's number. Which showed how grown up he really was.

Trish answered on the first ring. "Hello?"

"Hey," he said, keeping his voice low. "It's me. You won't believe what happened."

He heard her gasp. "Did he say yes?"

"Not yet, but wait till you hear this." He quickly told her about finding Abby and her kids on the county road. "I brought her home with me."

"You brought her home with you," Trish repeated, not sounding as pleased as he thought she'd be. "Why?"

"I couldn't leave her there, not with those little kids."

"Is she pretty?"

"Yeah, for an older woman. Uncle Jed sure noticed."

"How could you tell?"

"He stared at her."

"Really?"

"Yeah. And he said it was okay for Bull to take a look at her car."

"Cool," Trish agreed. "But what are you so excited about?"

"That engine was a piece of, uh, crap, honey. Smoke coming out, hotter than heck."

"So?"

"She's stuck here. For now, anyway. She's Uncle Jed's age. She's pretty. And she's nice."

"And?"

"Remember when you said that Uncle Jed needs to get a life? Well, I think this is it." He paused, then announced triumphantly, "I think I've found a woman for Jed."

THE "WOMAN FOR JED" was at that moment peeling a squirming baby off her lap.

"Here, honey, sit beside me for a minute." Abby stood her between her knees and let the child stretch. Abby watched Cass and Matt play a strange version of tag in the grassy area under an empty clothesline. They looked happy to be out of the car for a while, so at least there was one advantage to an overheated van. A breeze lifted Chrissie's yellow curls and cooled Abby's skin. She hoped she could be on her way soon. She didn't even want to think about how much it would cost, because then she would cry. And crying wasn't going to help a bit.

Ty poked his head out of the screen door. "Ma'am?"

Abby smiled at him. "Hi. I thought you'd be fixing that fence."

"Nah." He stepped out onto the porch and sat on the neighboring bench. "I'll do it later."

"You're not in trouble, then?"

"Not about that." He smiled at Chrissie, who clapped her chubby hands with excitement. He held out his arms to her. "You want to come with me and see the cows?"

"Ow?"

"She's shy sometimes," Abby explained, expecting her daughter to shriek. Then the baby reached for the young cowboy. "But I guess this isn't one of those times."

He put her on his lap. "I'll take the kids over to the corral for a few minutes. It's cooler in the house, ma'am, if you want to sit inside and drink a Coke."

"I'll go with you," Abby said, unwilling to let the children out of her sight. This young man didn't realize how quickly a child could get into trouble. "I wouldn't mind walking for a while myself."

"Great. The Gem is a pretty big ranch, one of the oldest in the state. You ever been to Wyoming before?"

"Not until today." She called Matt and Cass over to them and told them to stay beside her while they visited the cows.

Ty led them toward a large corral. "Well, this is God's country, ma'am. And ranching is a hard way to make a living, but I wouldn't want to do anything else."

"You work for your uncle?"

"I sure do. He's lived here all his life. This place *is* his life, but I don't think that's real healthy."

Abby couldn't help smiling. "You don't?"

"No, ma'am," Ty said, his voice serious despite the fact that Chrissie was pulling on his hat brim. "He works too hard. He works all the time, like he doesn't know that there's anything else to do. You know, for fun."

"There must be a lot to do around here." Everywhere she looked there were fences, corrals, out-buildings, machinery, and the occasional man dressed in denim and work boots.

Ty nodded. "Yep. More than usual since Old Walt died."

"I'm sorry. Who was Old Walt?"

"The cook. He was almost ninety, but he could still cook okay. We've all been taking turns since then." He stopped at the fence. "Now here are some pretty calves."

The children were thrilled, the calves were petrified and the young man explained that the calves weren't used to hearing children call out to them. "They'll come back to this end of the corral," he assured everyone. "They're real curious about everything, so if you hold still they'll come closer."

"If you can get these three to hold still, then you're some kind of miracle worker," Abby whispered.

"I like kids," Ty said. "I'd like five or six of my own someday."

Abby laughed. "I hope you find a woman who agrees with you."

"Oh, I have already, ma'am. We're going to get married as soon as we can."

She didn't point out that he was awfully young for such a big step. Who was she to give advice? Wounded divorcées were the last people qualified to make comments on marriage. "See that building over there? The two-story one with the blue door?" He pointed toward another cluster of outbuildings, all of which could use a fresh coat of white paint. The one Ty described sat off to one side and looked like something that would blow down during the next storm.

"Yes."

"That's where we're going to live when we get married. It's not real big, but it will do. We can always add on."

Abby had to admire the young man's enthusiasm. "You certainly have it all figured out."

"Well," he said, digging one booted toe in the dirt. "I've been thinking about it for a long time."

A long time? He couldn't be older than twenty, if he was even that. Abby suddenly felt every bit of her thirty-four years...and more. She hoped the boy's dream of a happy future would come true. "That's very nice," was all she could think to say. Who was she to step on anyone's dreams?

He adjusted his grip on the baby. "Want to see the hogs?"

"Sure," Abby said, taking Cass's hand and leading her from the calves. Matt climbed down from the fence and joined them.

"Don't stick your hands in the pen," Ty warned them.

"Hogs bite?" Matt asked.

"They can take your fingers right off if they feel like it."

Abby watched Matt shove his hands into his pockets as they walked down the road to the hog pen. She kept a firm hold on Cass's hand and made sure she kept an eye on Chrissie, who seemed to be very content to stay in Ty's arms and clutch his shoulder.

They stared at the fat hogs, admired the chickens, waved at the horses and kicked dust along the wide roads that wound around the many buildings. The constant breeze kept Abby from feeling the effects of the heat, but Ty's cheerful conversation couldn't prevent her from worrying about her van. Aside from her traveling money, she had one thousand seven hundred and three dollars to her name, and she would need every penny of it to get the family settled in Spokane.

This was no time for bad news, but when Abby saw a wizened cowboy walk toward them, she had the feeling that what she was about to hear wasn't going to be good.

The man tipped his hat toward her and spoke to Ty. "Block's cracked. Gonna need a new engine." Bull spit in the dust. "Dunno if it's worth it, though. That van is pretty darn old, doesn't look like it's worth saving."

"You sure?" Ty asked, while the words "not worth saving" rang in Abby's ears.

The man shrugged. "I gave it the once-over pretty good. Can't do much more without taking the whole thing apart, and that'd take hours. And I'd have to put the thing in the shop for that."

Abby took a deep breath. "How much would it cost to fix it?"

"You'd be better off taking your money and buying something else. Least, that's one man's opinion."

Ty nodded. "Thanks, Bull. I appreciate it."

"Yes," Abby added. "Thank you so much."

"You want me to tow it in here for now? Probably shouldn't be on the road overnight."

"I don't know. I guess I'll have to—"

"Mommy." Cass tugged on her hand. "I hafta go to the bathroom."

"Help yourself," Ty said. "Go through the kitchen and it's on the right."

Abby took Chrissie out of his arms. She didn't know what to do next. Ask this nice young man for a ride to town? Find a motel, a phone book, another car and a place to buy lottery tickets? "I'm sorry to be taking up so much of your time, but is there any way I can get a ride to the nearest town?"

"Sure, Abby. I'll be inside in a minute."

She paused. "Thanks, Ty. I appreciate it." She herded the children toward the main house as quickly as she could. She opened the screen door and stepped into a large kitchen that desperately needed a good scrubbing. Dirty dishes were piled in stacks on the counters and, in the center of the room, a long table needed to be wiped off. Obviously Ty's uncle wasn't married, or if he was his wife didn't believe in cleanliness.

"Messy," Cass declared, wrinkling her nose.

"Yes," her mother agreed. "*Very* messy."

Matt's eyes were wide as he looked around. "There's a *saddle* on the floor," he whispered.

"It's not polite to snoop," she warned him, but she couldn't help looking around the kitchen. If she had ever wondered what a cowboy's kitchen looked like, she didn't have to wonder any longer. Liniment and bandages sat on one of the oak chairs, shirts draped from others. She smelled meat roasting in the large oven, though, so at least someone around here cooked.

"Mommy, I hafta go. Now."

"Sure." Abby wondered what the bathroom would look like. Now there was a scary thought. She led her children out of the kitchen to a wide hallway. Just as Ty had said, there was a small bathroom off to the right. Abby hesitated, but Cass ran right in and shut the door, leaving the rest of the family out in the hall.

"This is really neat," her son said, peering around the corner of the living room. "Look at the TV!"

Abby set Chrissie on her feet and held on to her hands. "Matt, don't go any farther."

He stopped, but his gaze swept the living room. "There's a bear on the floor!"

"That must be a bearskin rug," she told him. From where she stood she saw a black leather recliner and the edge of a braided rug. A painting of a mountain hung on the pine-paneled wall behind the chair.

"I'm done!" Cass announced as she opened the door. Abby peered inside, hoping that the bathroom was cleaner than the kitchen. It was, to the point of looking unused. "Did you wash your hands?"

"Yes. With blue soap."

"Matt, it's your turn."

"I don't hafta go."

"Go anyway."

He reluctantly returned to his mother and went into the bathroom. When he was done, Abby told her eldest children to stand *right there* and not move while she used the bathroom, too. She took the baby with her and used the opportunity to wash the child's face and hands, plus splash water on her own. That would have to do until she found a motel for the evening. Maybe after a hot shower and a good night's sleep she could make a decision about how to get to Spokane without a car.

Maybe everything would look better in the morning.

JED WATCHED the little family head toward the house. The woman didn't look happy, which meant that van of hers must have given up the fight. Guess that meant he'd have to spare Ty a while longer while he took those people into town. He stepped out of the barn and headed toward Ty to give him some instructions, instructions that would include not stopping at the Jensen place on his way back from Carson.

"Well?"

Bull shook his head. "That vehicle's shot, unless the lady wants to put another engine in it."

"Too bad."

"She's a looker," the mechanic said.

Ty grinned. "Yeah," he agreed. "A looker."

The man winked at the younger Monroe. "Wonder if she can cook. Food around here ain't been the same these past months."

Jed felt an unspoken conversation going on around him. "I put an ad in the paper. It's not my fault that no one's called for the job." There weren't a lot of people willing to work so far away from town and even fewer who wanted to live in the middle of ranch country.

"I miss having biscuits for breakfast." Bull sighed and wiped his greasy hands on a rag. "Life just ain't been the same."

Ty nodded. "You know, you might just have something there. Maybe you should offer Abby, uh, Mrs. Andrews, a job, Uncle Jed."

"Maybe you've been out in the sun without your hat."

"She's got kids. That means she can cook," Ty insisted.

"I'm looking for a man for the job."

"Why?"

"Because." He didn't have to explain anything to a scrawny teenager, especially about women. "This is no place for women."

Bull guffawed. "Don't remember any being here these past ten years, so I can't recollect. Don't think you'd hear any of the men griping about the cooking long as they could talk to a lady."

Ty couldn't hide his laughter. "Why don't you like women, Uncle Jed?"

Jed frowned. "I like women. Just not here."

"When's the last time you had a date?"

"None of your business."

His nephew put his hands on his hips. "You keep telling me I should start taking on more responsibility around here, don't you?"

"Yeah. But that doesn't mean you have the right to tell me how I'm supposed to run things."

Bull took a step backward. "I'd better work on the tractor," he muttered.

Jed called to him. "You sure that van can't be fixed?"

"Yeah. You want me to tow it in?"

"I'll ask the lady." He turned back to his nephew. "You can ask Mrs. Andrews if she needs any more help."

"I don't think she has a lot of money. She looked pretty upset about the car."

"That doesn't mean she wants or needs a job, Ty."

He shrugged. "It was just an idea. Thought I could solve two problems at once."

Jed relented and clapped the boy on the shoulder. "Don't take this so seriously, son. For all we know, that woman has a great big Visa card and a husband who'll come running to the rescue the minute she calls him."

"She wasn't wearing a ring."

He'd noticed that, too. Right after he'd noticed those full breasts and tanned legs. Mrs. Andrews had an enticing little body and a sweet smile, which were two attributes a ranch cook shouldn't possess. Jed needed someone tough. Someone used to hard work. Someone who would not be intimidated by four ranch hands every day. Someone, well, male. "You're not responsible for her, Ty."

He grinned. "But I found her."

"And you helped her," he said, moving toward the house. "Now it's time to help her to get to town. She's no kid. She'll figure it out."

"She's a good-looking woman."

Jed chuckled. "I won't argue with you there."

Ty stayed silent until they reached the house. "It's almost suppertime. Let's give them something to eat before I take them to town. There'll still be enough light left to tow the van."

Jed sighed. "Go ahead, then. Feed them. I've got some things to do outside, so don't wait supper on me."

"You're not going to eat with us?"

"You made pot roast again?"

"Yeah."

"It'll keep, then. I'll tell the men to come in when they want and help themselves." Jed turned to leave, but Ty stopped him.

"And what about Mrs. Andrews?"

"Help her as much as you can, Ty, but don't forget you still have fence to check."

His nephew looked pleased with himself. "No problem, Uncle Jed. I'll get right on it."

"Good." Maybe the boy would start paying more attention to his work now that he'd been told he couldn't get married.

He stopped inside the barn door and took a beer from the old refrigerator. He took a long swallow from the bottle and leaned against the door frame.

"Boss?"

He looked up to see Toby and Bull in the doorway. "Yeah?"

"We're finished."

"Good. Ty's made supper, so go help yourself."

Jed opened his mouth to warn them about the guests, but then changed his mind. They'd find out soon enough.

"You comin'?"

Jed shook his head. "I'll be along later," he promised.

After the lady left.

3

ABBY CLOSED the telephone book. Despite trains, planes and buses, the Andrews family and all their possessions were stuck in Wyoming until she could figure out how to fix her van or buy another.

Her mother would say, "I told you so." She didn't have to make a call to Spokane to hear the words. And since she had resolved to stand on her own two feet from now on, she was not going to go running to her mother for help the first time something went wrong.

"Ma'am?"

She looked up as Ty slid a plateful of food beside her. "Oh, Ty, thank you, but—"

"It's suppertime. You and the kids should eat." He plopped a handful of silverware on the table. "Help yourself. We're not real formal around here."

"You've been so kind." She stopped Chrissie from grabbing a fork and gave her a spoon to play with instead. She shifted her over to her left side. "I don't know what to say."

"You don't have to say anything." He put glasses of milk and smaller plates in front of Cass and Matt, who sat across the table from her and were uncharacteristically silent. "Does the baby drink milk, too?"

"I'll fix her a bottle after supper, if that's okay with you."

"We've got lots of milk. Don't worry about that."

Two stocky, weathered ranch hands entered the kitchen, saw the children and hesitated before coming any closer.

"It's ready," Ty assured them. "Come on in."

They glanced at Abby and quickly removed their hats. One was the man who had taken Mr. Monroe's horse. The other was the man who had looked at her van. Both men were bald, with light foreheads and ruddy cheeks.

"Pot roast," one of them said. "Should have known."

Ty waved them toward the stove. "Yeah, well, it's all I know how to cook."

The older man chuckled. "It's all that's left in the freezer."

"Toby, Bull, this is Mrs. Andrews and her kids."

"It's very nice to meet you," Abby said. "Thank you again for your help, Mr., uh, Bull."

"Ma'am," they said in unison. She wondered if they were brothers.

Matt stared as the men helped themselves from a large pan on the counter. "Is Bull your real name?"

"Cowboys have nicknames, son," one replied. "What's yours?"

"I'm just Matt."

"No nickname?"

"No."

"Well," the man drawled, taking the seat beside the boy. He winked at Abby, then turned to the child. "Guess you'd better get one."

"How?"

"You have to do something special."

"Aw, Bull, you know that's not—"

"Now don't go interrupting, Toby. Just because your name's 'Tobias' doesn't mean Toby ain't a good nickname."

Toby sat down, leaving an empty seat between Abby and himself. She supposed he was shy. Obviously the Gem didn't get a lot of female visitors. "I once rode a bull," Bull continued, "that was so mean he could bite off his own tail and not care. But I rode him, until the buzzer went off—this was in the Cheyenne Rodeo, back in the days when it was just starting to get famous—and then I was s'posed to jump off and let them rodeo clowns take over." He paused to eat a large forkful of beef, while his young audience waited silently for him to continue.

"Jeez," Toby complained, stabbing a forkful of beef. "Let's kill a couple of chickens tomorrow. I'm gonna grow horns and moo pretty soon."

Matt leaned forward. "Then what happened, Mr. Bull?"

"Well," the cowboy said, clearly enjoying himself. "I couldn't get off that darn animal. Not for all the money in the world. I think my hand froze to the leather or somethin'." He shrugged. "Those clowns were running all around doin' that clown stuff, you know, and there I was just riding and riding that bull and he was snortin' and jumpin' and pretty soon the crowd was screaming and cheering and going plumb wild."

"You ever think you might have the name 'Bull' for another reason?" Toby asked.

Bull winked across the table at Abby. "I don't know how long I rode that mean old bull, but the sun went down and the lights around the arena came on and there we were, sawdust coming up everywhere like a snowstorm in December." He stabbed a chunk of potato. "And folks have called me 'Bull' ever since, in honor of that ride. *That*'s one way to get a nickname, son."

"Cool."

Ty grinned as he sat down at the table with a plate piled high with food in front of him. "You sure do have a way with words."

Cass didn't smile. "Are there mean old bulls on this ranch?"

"He—heck yes, little lady," Toby answered. "But they're miles from here. And nobody rides them, not even old Bull here."

"That's good," the little girl said.

"I wish I had a nickname." Matt finished his dinner and looked at the cowboys. "Can you give me one?"

Bull leaned back and rubbed his chin. "Well, I'll consider the question," he said. "But I can't promise anything. You know how to work?"

Abby fed Chrissie a small spoonful of potato and waited for the answer.

"Uh, sure," her son replied. "I can vacuum."

Bull nodded. "Real useful skill. Might be hard to get a nickname out of that, though."

Cass giggled. "I call him Matt the Rat."

"Least I don't have a dumb name like Cassandra Louise," he muttered.

"I'll give it some thought," the old cowboy promised. "You folks heading out soon?"

"Yes," Abby said, trying to keep the knife away from the baby's chubby fingers. Right now she would have given a lot for the high chair folded up in the back of her van. "I just have to figure out how."

"Where're you headed?"

"Spokane."

"Well, you could probably hook up with a bus that would go there."

"Almost everything we own is in that van. I don't know what I'd do with it all."

"Ship it?"

"I might have to." She took Chrissie's fingers out of the potatoes and mashed a piece of carrot for her. "Is there any place around here where I could buy a cheap used car?"

"Begging your pardon, ma'am, but do you think that's real wise?" Toby cleared his throat. "You might be trading one set of problems for another, and the next time you broke down you might not be where folks could help you."

The man had a point. Abby tried to smile. "I

know you're right, but at this point I think I'm going to have to take the chance. Either that, or get a job in Wyoming until I earn enough money for a decent car."

"You could be a cowboy, Mom," her daughter suggested.

Abby shook her head. "I'm afraid I don't know how to be a cowboy."

Bull chuckled. "No, ma'am. I'm guessing you ain't done much ropin' and ridin' in your day, and you don't look strong enough to do any hayin', either."

"I'm afraid not," she replied. "But I will pay for my supper by washing the dishes. If you'll let me, that is."

Bull leaned forward. "Can you cook, ma'am? Pardon my askin', but this is the nineties, and some women *don't* cook these days. Hard as that is to believe," he added, his expression solemn.

"I can cook," Abby replied, trying to keep from laughing.

"Mom makes really good cookies," Matt volunteered.

Toby nudged Ty. "We could sure use a cook around here."

"I'm not looking for a job," Abby said, wondering as the words came out of her mouth if that was something she needed to think about. "But I'll be glad to pay for my supper by cleaning up the kitchen."

"You will?" Ty asked, looking relieved. "I

mean, it's my night to clean up, but it doesn't have to get done right away."

"Let me help," she urged.

Ty grinned. "I sure can't refuse that."

No man in his right mind would, Abby knew. She would fix a bottle for the baby and tackle this mess. She didn't have a lot of money, but she sure knew how to wash dishes. And she had some thinking to do. About her van. About her future. About her bank account.

Besides, Abby thought, carrying a stack of dirty plates to the counter, she did some of her best thinking when she was cleaning.

HE HOPED they were gone. There was something about that woman, something about the sad look in her eyes and the way she'd refused to fall apart when told her old van wasn't worth fixing. There was something about her that made him want to protect her, take her into his arms and tell her that everything would be all right.

And that boy. He reminded Jed of Ty at that age. There was a lost look on his face, like he was between lives. Like he didn't know where he was going and didn't know what he'd find when he got there.

No, he hoped by now that they were on their way. Ty would have taken them into town and would have forgotten all about that fence line. He'd spend the evening with Trish, if her father wasn't around to kick him off the place. And he'd come home talking about getting married and playing house in one of the old bunkhouses. The kid thought that all his troubles would be over if he could just get married.

Jed walked slowly toward the house. He didn't need the complications that women brought to ranch life. Hell, he was still reeling eleven years after Johnny's death. Before Patty died, his brother's headstrong and spoiled young wife had caused so much trouble on the Gem that Jed still winced when he thought about her. She'd been driving the night their car crashed into an oncoming truck. They'd both been too drunk to know what hit them.

No, Ty should never have brought another woman here. He hoped they were gone.

They weren't. He noticed her right away. She had her back to him, her arms elbow-deep in dishwater. Dishes were piled everywhere and, most miraculous of all, the long dinner table was empty, its surface scrubbed clean.

"What the hell are you doing?"

She jumped a little and turned her head to see him. "You scared me."

"Sorry."

"I'm trying to help."

"It's Ty's job to do that."

She turned back to the sink and started scrubbing again. "I offered."

"We have a dishwasher."

"It's full. Besides, no machine could get this stuff off." She held up a dripping pan. "I don't know what this was, but I hope you didn't have to eat it."

"Not much goes to waste around here," was all he think of to say. He stood inside the room and didn't know what to do. He was hungry, he was tired, and there was still an hour or two of daylight left, so he didn't have time to waste talking about dirty dishes.

"You haven't eaten," the woman said. "I fixed you a plate. It's in the refrigerator."

"You fixed me a plate," he repeated without moving. She wiped her hands on a towel and opened the refrigerator, removed a dinner plate and put it in the microwave oven. Jed stood by the door for the full two minutes that the food was heating. The woman removed it from the oven and walked over to the table, where she set it down. "I'll get you some silverware."

"I can—"

"No," she said, but she smiled as her gaze met his. "I'm trying to repay your hospitality, you see."

"That's not—"

"Of course it is," she replied, not giving him time to protest. "Sit down and eat while I finish up here."

He managed to move across the room and take his customary seat at the foot of the table, the one that faced the television in the corner. The television was on, he noticed, the volume low as dancing puppets flickered on the screen. He saw the children for the first time. They sat on the floor and leaned against Ty's roping saddle, the baby asleep on a pink blanket between them.

"I guess you eat a lot of pot roast," the woman said, giving him a set of silverware still warm from the washing.

"Yes." He moved his plate closer. Pot roast, carrots and chunks of potatoes were no surprise here on the Gem.

"I heard your cook died."

"Yes. Good man. Buried in town behind Murphy's Bar."

"Well. That's…nice." She twisted the towel in her hands as she stood by the table. "Mr. Monroe, I have a proposition for you."

He looked up at her and almost put down his fork, but he was hungry and the meal was decent, so he held on to it and waited for the woman to explain herself. "Ma'am?"

"Please call me Abby. I've been called 'ma'am' so much today that I'm starting to feel as old as your, um, former cook."

He didn't want a "proposition." He wanted to eat his supper and then he wanted to work with the new roan mare. But he didn't want to be rude, so he gestured toward the empty seat near him. "Abby," he said, though he didn't like the familiarity. "What kind of proposition?"

She blushed. No, her cheeks were flushed from the steaming dishwater. Women her age didn't blush. "Do you *like* eating the same dinner every night?"

"Well, I—"

"I mean," she said, sitting in the offered chair, "I think you need another cook. Someone to run this kitchen. Someone like me."

"Like you."

She met his gaze. "I need a job and you need a cook. I'm applying for the job."

"I thought you were heading west."

"I was, until today. I need to earn money for another car."

He considered loaning her the money, but then he came to his senses. She was a stranger. Pretty, yes. And proud. He could respect that, but that didn't mean that he should write her a check. And what was a woman like her doing crossing the country with no money?

"I realize you don't know me," she continued, still twisting the towel in her lap. "And I don't blame you if you don't want to hire me, but I've been cooking for my family for ten years and I know how to put a meal together."

"I don't doubt—"

"I'm a hard worker. I don't drink—oh, except maybe a glass of wine socially, but I haven't had much time to be social lately—and I don't smoke. Not even cigars."

"Cigars?" He put his fork down, figuring this "proposition" was going to take longer than he thought.

"You know. It's a big fad in Hollywood now. All the movie stars are doing it, and I even read that there are cigar bars around the country, with nights for women. But never mind that. You can smoke them if you want to, after all it's your house, but I think it's a disgusting habit."

"I don't—"

"You can if you want. You're the boss. Which is the whole point. I mean, I can cook, that's all that matters."

"But the kids—"

"Won't bother anyone," she assured him. "I'll make sure of it. I can do my work, just the way I used to at home. I have a high chair and a playpen in the van, and I'll make sure Cass and Matt don't bother anybody outside."

"This is a working ranch," he stated, pleased that he could finally finish a sentence. That dish towel was sure to tear in two from the way she twisted it.

"Yes," she said, and then looked at him as though she was waiting for him to say something. He figured she must have finally run out of breath.

"This isn't a real money-making job, Mrs.—"

"Andrews." She leaned forward, the dish towel wound tight around one small hand. "What did you pay Walt?"

"Not much."

Her face fell, but she quickly smiled to hide her disappointment.

"Course, he got room and board," Jed explained, wondering why he was defending the job. Did he really want to hire this woman? No, he didn't. Not at all.

Her smile stayed firmly in place. "I guess Old Walt didn't need a car."

He wished she wouldn't look at him like that. He hoped she wasn't going to cry. "No."

"Did he clean and do laundry?"

"Uh, no. Not really."

"I would."

"How much would you want?" he asked, fully expecting her to name an unreasonable sum so he could, in good conscience, turn her down. Where in blazes had Ty gone off to? He should have taken this family to Carson by now.

"I need a car that will get me where I want to go. How much do you think that will cost?"

"Lady, I wouldn't have any idea." Women were strange creatures. Did they think men knew *everything?* Jed took a deep breath. "What kind of car did you have in mind?"

"I don't care what kind, as long as it will get me to Spokane without breaking down."

"You might want to look in the local paper. Don't you have any money?"

She shook her head. "Not enough to buy a car and get an apartment. I can probably sell the van, don't you think?"

"Possibly. You might get something for it."

"Good. How does four hundred a week sound?"

"Like highway robbery. Two hundred was all I paid Old Walt, and he was happy."

She shrugged. "He didn't clean. Or wash

clothes. Three hundred. With Sundays off and use of a car to go to town once a week."

He should have stopped it right then, before visions of dinner plates piled high with something other than pot roast filled his head. He should have put his fork down and driven her to town himself. Instead he glanced over at the kids curled up in front of his television set. Hell. They were practically homeless.

"All right," he heard himself say as he turned back to face his new employee. "You've got a deal, but you'd better know how to cook."

"I won't disappoint you, Mr. Monroe," she promised, and the battered dish towel was tossed over her shoulder as she stood and held out her hand for him to shake.

"I hope not, Mrs. Andrews," was about all he could manage to say as he held her hand for one brief second. "Can I eat my supper now?"

"Certainly." She turned toward the sink, but stopped and faced him again. "You said room and board was included?"

He sighed and put down his fork. "Yes, ma'am."

"Where exactly is the room?"

"Take your pick for tonight, Mrs. Andrews. There are four empty bedrooms upstairs. If you poke around in the closets you can find everything you need. You can move your things into a bunkhouse tomorrow, but you're going to want to clean the place up first."

"And my van?"

"I'll have one of the men tow it here, if that's what you want."

"That would probably be best. Thank you."

"You're welcome." Jed picked up his fork and pierced a cold potato.

"Do you want—"

"Mrs. Andrews, if you ask me one more question you're fired."

"I was going to offer to heat up your dinner again."

He didn't know if she was going to laugh or cry, but he sure didn't want to take any chances on the crying part. Jed shook his head. "I'm fine."

His new cook went back to washing dishes, which gave Jed a disconcerting view of a trim backside and a tiny waist emphasized by apron ties. Nice legs, too, if a man liked petite women. Which he didn't. Abby Andrews looked like she would break easily, and that kind of woman made him nervous. He ate the rest of his supper in silence, except for the churning of the dishwasher and the banging of pots and pans in the sink. Every once in a while he looked at the kids, but they never moved from their makeshift bed on the floor. The baby slept through it all, her thumb in her mouth and her fist curled against her nose.

He finished his supper and pushed his plate aside. Mrs. Andrews poured a cup of coffee and placed it in front of him.

"I won't ask if you take anything in it," she said.

"Good."

She removed his dirty dishes and plopped them in the sink. "You don't have to wait on me," he said, but he secretly enjoyed the service. Maybe this would be worth three hundred a week after all.

"That's what I'm getting paid to do." She sounded cheerful, but he couldn't see her face. She was washing dishes again. He saw that the counters were cleared off. First time in months for that to happen. He took a sip of his coffee. She'd made it strong—another good sign.

"You have a bear in your house," came a whisper near his elbow.

"Where?"

"In there." The little girl pointed toward the living room. "Matt told me. He peeked. I didn't."

A bear in the living room? Then he remembered. "Ah, the rug. My grandfather shot that bear a long time ago. He can't hurt you."

"Show me?" She put her hand out for him to take, so Jed could hardly refuse.

"Cass," her mother said. "Leave Mr. Monroe alone."

"It's okay," he assured her. The child's tiny fingers curled around two of his as he led her through the living room and toward the fireplace. "There. See? Flat as can be."

She dug her heels into the carpet and stopped. "It's got a *head*."

"Uh, well, that's how you know it's a bear."

"Oh." But she didn't move. "But it doesn't bite?"

He hesitated. Would she cry if he used the word *dead*? "No. It can't move. It's, uh, like a teddy bear. A very flat teddy bear."

The little girl stared up at him. "Really, truly?"

"You want to feel it and find out for yourself?"

"Uh-uh." She let go of his hand and backed out of the room. "It's scary here."

He followed her back to the kitchen, to his clean sparkling kitchen and the sound of a woman humming a song as she scrubbed the stove top.

Scary? Damn right it was.

4

"SHE'S STAYING," Ty announced. He waited for Trish to tell him how smart he was and, sure enough, she smiled and walked into his arms. Boy, was he glad her father wasn't home.

"How did you do it?" she asked.

He kissed her before he answered. "I'll tell you later."

Trish shook her head and took his hand. She led him toward her house. "Tell me now. I don't want to wait."

"I don't want to wait, either." But he was talking about something else and she knew it.

"First you have to tell me everything," Trish insisted. They went inside the tiny two-story house and headed straight for the living room. Trish curled up on the couch and Ty sat close to her.

"I don't know much, just what Uncle Jed told me." He bent to kiss her.

"Which was?" she prompted.

Ty sighed. "That Mrs. Andrews was going to stay on for a while and cook. I'm glad, too, 'cause I'm real tired of eating the same food all the time. Anyway, we towed her van to the ranch. I guess she doesn't have much money to buy a new one."

"That must be awful for her."

"Yeah. She's real nice, and so are her kids. You wouldn't believe how clean the kitchen is already."

"That place was a mess," she agreed. "I'm surprised your uncle didn't hire anyone before now."

"He tried. Not too many people were interested."

"Do you think she'll need help?"

"Huh?" Ty loved that pink shirt Trish wore. And those white shorts were going to make him crazy.

"Mrs. Andrews. Will she need help? A babysitter?"

He pulled his gaze away from Trish's bare legs and tried to remember what she'd asked. "Babysitter?"

"Gee, Ty, are you falling asleep?"

"Nope. What are you getting at?"

Trish smiled at him, but he ignored the ache in his groin and concentrated real hard on her words. "I could help with the kids whenever Dad didn't need me. I could ride over sometimes and, you know, baby-sit."

"Now who's smart?"

"Both of us," she declared, leaning over to kiss his mouth. "If your uncle sees that we're happy together, he'll have to change his mind. Maybe he should get to know me better."

Ty hoped she was right. They were going to get married whether or not Uncle Jed approved, but it would be a whole lot easier for everyone if his uncle was on their side. "When's your dad coming home?"

"Late." She smiled. "*Very* late."

"Wow," Ty said. "This is turning into a really good day."

ABBY WAS NOT where she had expected to be tonight, but a creaky metal bed in a Wyoming ranch house was much better than being stranded on the side of a gravel road, and she was grateful for it.

She couldn't believe how she'd talked to Mr. Monroe. Couldn't believe the words that had come from her lips and the way she'd pretended to be brave while she'd talked him into hiring her. All the while her hands had been shaking so badly she'd had to grip the damp dish towel to keep from showing how nervous she was. Thank goodness the tall rancher hadn't noticed. He had hired her. She had talked him into it, all right. She hadn't known she could be such a bully.

And she now had a job to do. A job was what she needed, so why couldn't she sleep? A million worries went 'round and 'round in her head. What time would the meals have to be ready. What did they like for breakfast? What did they expect for lunch? Where would she find a grocery store, and how much food should she cook for each meal? Jed Monroe had given her the job, but he hadn't given her any instructions. Surely tomorrow he would give her an idea what he expected from his new cook. She would write out a list of questions for the next time she saw him.

He seemed like such a quiet man. Those dark eyes of his didn't miss anything, though. He'd sized her up in one look, and if she didn't know better she'd think he was afraid. No one had ever been afraid of her before, so Abby knew she was mistaken about that impression. She wondered if he ever laughed, since he barely smiled. And yet he didn't look mean. He looked like a man who worked long and hard and didn't take much time off to relax. He looked like the hero of every Western movie she'd ever seen.

He'd left the house after dinner, taking his coffee with him. She had spent the evening unpacking the van and settling the children into their new home. The rooms upstairs were small and sparse, with beds, dressers and dust-filled braided rugs. Each contained a walk-in closet and a window overlooking some part of the ranch. There was a bathroom on the second floor, but it appeared as unused as the rest of the upstairs. She'd found linens in a hall closet; she'd made up two twin beds for Matt and Cass in one room, then taken the room beside them for her own. By pushing the double bed against the wall, she'd made it safe for Chrissie to sleep beside her and not fall out.

Now, with everyone settled for the night, there was nothing left to do but sleep. Abby didn't know why that was so hard to do. She yearned for peace. She'd spent the last months making decisions, writing lists, packing boxes, having yard sales. She'd sold her house and had managed not to say one bitter word when her ex-husband took his half of the profits and left for Puerto Vallarta with his new bride. She'd paid legal bills with hers.

She'd tried to be a good person, but it hadn't been easy. Visions of revenge had been comforting, but Greg was still the children's father. Even if he'd said he was tired of the responsibilities and the "sameness of it all."

Well, there was no more of that "sameness" for any member of the Andrews family. Their possessions were in storage, their future home had yet to be found and rented, and they had spent the last week on the road chugging along from one inexpensive motel to the next. She'd budgeted carefully; she'd had no other options.

Until now. When the only option left was to stop and earn some money. She would call her mother and tell her that she was going to spend the summer with friends, that she would arrive in Spokane later on in the fall. Cora would fuss. She hadn't approved of the divorce, hadn't approved of the move, hadn't approved of much of anything Abby did for the past twenty years. Abby smiled to herself in the darkness. At least she was taking care of her family, no matter what disasters had crashed down upon them.

She closed her eyes and listened to the comforting sound of her baby's light breathing. The window was open and a horse nickered softly, but otherwise there was only silence. Abby told herself to go to sleep, that tomorrow morning would come soon enough, but she worried over menus and supplies until she finally drifted off.

HE THOUGHT he was dreaming, until he heard someone calling a warning. Jed jumped out of bed and grabbed the rifle he kept hung on the wall above his bureau.

"Bear!" came the high-pitched voice again, and Jed swore under his breath. It wasn't unheard of to see a grizzly in this part of the country, but it wasn't a normal occurrence, either. He hurried out to the kitchen and peered out the back door. He didn't want any surprises, so he listened for a long moment.

"Bull? Toby?" he whispered, hoping one of the old cowhands would answer. Nothing stirred outside, so Jed started back down the hall to his bed. He felt a little foolish, until another scream split the silence.

Upstairs he heard footsteps and muffled voiced, so he took the stairs two at a time and hurried to the room where light spilled out of the doorway.

"What the hell—" Jed stopped when the little girl screamed at the sight of him.

Abby folded the child into her arms. "She's having a nightmare. I'm so sorry we woke you."

"A nightmare?"

Cass looked at him with huge eyes that glistened with tears. "There was a *bear* in my room."

"The rug," Abby explained. "I guess it really scared her."

"Is she okay?"

"She'll settle down in a minute." Abby stared at his arm. "Is that *loaded*? Do you have loaded weapons in this house?"

Jed felt pretty ridiculous as he remembered the rifle in his hand. "Yes, ma'am, but I'll put it in a safe place first thing in the morning."

Matt sat up in his bed and stared at everyone. "What's going on? Are you going to shoot something?"

"Uh, no," he assured the child. "I thought there was a—" He didn't want to say the word "bear" and scare the little girl again.

"See?" Abby comforted her daughter. "Mr. Monroe will protect you from any wild animals."

"He will? He's not wearing any pajamas," the child said, sniffing.

And Jed remembered that he wore only a pair of boxer shorts. He backed out of the room. "Sorry, ma'am. I didn't stop to think—"

He thought he heard her apologize as he hurried back down the hall to the stairs that would take him closer to his own bed. A nightmare had sent him running around the house in his underwear, which was downright embarrassing. She would think he was some kind of pervert, waving a rifle and walking around half naked in the middle of the night.

Jed hung up the rifle and climbed into bed. He was too old for this kind of excitement, but unfortunately a man was never too old to look like a fool.

And considering he'd just talked to a woman who wasn't wearing much more than a long T-shirt, he realized how long it had been since he'd spoken to a lady in the middle of the night. He had no business thinking about the woman like that, though, despite the memory of her bare legs and the swell of full breasts under the thin cotton material of her shirt. These summer nights could be cool. She should wear something like flannel.

It was a long time before he went back to sleep.

"YOU MUST HAVE BEEN pretty tired last night."

Ty looked up from his plate of bacon and eggs. "What?"

His uncle sipped his coffee. "Last night. You slept through all the excitement."

"I did?" Ty turned his attention back to his eggs. "I mean, I *did*, yeah. I was real tired."

"Yeah, that's what I figured."

Ty ate another forkful of Abby's fluffy scrambled eggs and waited for his uncle to continue, but when he couldn't stand the silence any longer, he had to ask, "So, what happened?"

"Maybe I should ask you that," his uncle said. "Where'd you disappear to last night?"

Abby returned to the kitchen with the baby on her hip and smiled at Ty. "How's your breakfast?"

"Real good, thanks," Ty replied, hoping she'd

keep talking. She looked real pretty, for a mother. He hoped Jed would notice that Abby had great legs and a pretty hot figure for a woman her age. How could any man not notice? It wasn't like Jed had hordes of women following him around the ranch. "I'm sure glad you're staying on for a while. Can I get you anything in town today?"

"I'm not sure," she said, settling the baby in a high chair near the counter. "I haven't gone through all the cupboards yet. But I'll let you know as soon as I get a list together."

"You're not going to town," Jed told him. "You're working, remember?"

"Yeah, but I thought later—"

"No. I figure I'll get a full day's work out of you today, son." Jed winked. "Since you had such a good night's sleep and all."

Ty didn't dare yawn. And he didn't look at his uncle, either, for fear he'd see that Jed knew he'd spent most of the night with Trish. "Sure. Whatever."

"I'm really sorry for all the noise last night," Abby said, pouring milk into a baby bottle. The little girl clapped her hands and giggled.

"I didn't hear any noise," Ty said truthfully. "What happened?"

"Cass thought the bearskin rug in your living room was alive and under her bed."

"She did? Wow. I remember being real nervous around that rug, too," Ty confessed. "I kept my feet away from those teeth."

Jed finished his coffee and stood. "Did she go back to sleep?"

"After a while," Abby assured him. "Would you like some more coffee? I just made a fresh pot."

"No, uh, thanks. The kids aren't awake?"

"No."

Ty, curious to see what his uncle would do next, pushed his empty plate aside. "Not everyone gets up at dawn, Uncle Jed."

His uncle clapped his hat on his head and walked toward the door. "You're the last one up around here. The rest of the men are already working. Come on, Ty. I've got a long list today."

He sighed and took his plate over to Abby. "Thanks for breakfast."

"You're very welcome. Mr. Monroe?"

Jed paused at the door. "Yes?"

"What time do you want lunch, and what would you like to eat?"

"Noon is fine, ma'am. And anything we can put between two pieces of bread is good enough. No one around here is real fussy."

"You don't require a hot meal?"

"Not unless you're getting rid of leftovers," he said, moving closer to the door. He looked like a man who wanted to run.

Ty paused to play peekaboo with Chrissie. She giggled again and waved her pudgy fists at him.

"Ty." Jed's voice was mild but it was enough to make Ty grab his hat and hurry to the kitchen door.

"I don't know why you're in such a hurry," he protested. "It's barely light out." He followed Jed across the yard. "I don't think the cattle are awake yet, either."

"Quit your griping." He stopped when he got to the barn. "We're always up this early."

"You usually read the paper and listen to the weather channel." Ty yawned. He couldn't help it. "You usually take your time."

"Well, I didn't feel like it this morning."

"Because of Abby?"

"Mrs. Andrews," Jed corrected.

"She asked me to call her 'Abby.'"

"I just felt like getting a good start this morning. Before it gets too hot. And I didn't want to talk about your sex life in front of Mrs. Andrews." He turned to face Ty, and his dark eyes were serious. "Where the hell were you last night?"

Ty didn't flinch. "With Trish."

"You think that's smart?"

"We're going to get married."

"That's not smart, either. You stay away from that girl before her old man catches on that the two of you aren't doing homework together anymore."

Ty balled his fists at his sides and stood his ground. "We're in love."

Jed sighed. "Hell, Ty, you're only nineteen. Could we go through one day without having this conversation?" Ty didn't answer. "Go on, get to work. I told Toby you'd help him with the irrigation up north today."

"All day?"

"That's right. You'd better take a couple of sandwiches with you."

It wouldn't do any good to argue. In fact, Ty decided, he would do as he was told. Might be a good idea to disappear for the day and avoid Jed's lectures. "Sure, but what about that fence?"

"You can do it after supper."

Instead of seeing Trish, was what his uncle meant. "You know, Uncle Jed, if you had a girlfriend yourself, you might see things differently." With that said, he put on his hat and headed toward the bunkhouse to find Toby. He'd been with Jed since his folks died, so he was used to dealing with the man. There hadn't been any other family except for a couple of distant cousins. From what he'd heard, his mom had been really beautiful but more of a city gal. And his dad had loved her so much he'd sold his share of the ranch, moved them to Casper and bought himself a John Deere dealership.

He understood that kind of love, but he was really glad Trish didn't want him to change. He was a lucky man to be able to stay here on the Gem. It was just about the only home he'd ever known. And someday he'd teach his own sons the same things Jed had taught him.

DAMN KID. So he thought his uncle needed a girlfriend. Jed stomped back to the house. Teenagers thought they knew it all. Forty-year-old men didn't have *girlfriends*, for Pete's sake. Especially forty-year-old men who lived forty miles from a town that was only populated by two thousand or so people. Not too many were single women under the age of forty and over twenty-one. Those that were already had somebody. There hadn't been an unattached single female in town since the postmaster's sister came to visit last fall, and she had turned out to be engaged to a truck driver in Casper.

He didn't want a girlfriend. He didn't want a wife. He sure wouldn't mind having sex once in a while, though, but he didn't need the complications women caused a man. Look at Ty, all tied up in knots over getting married, staying out half the night, yawning half the day and mooning around over the Jensen girl. Trish seemed like a decent kid, but Ty was too young to settle down, no matter whom he wanted to marry.

Jed stomped into the kitchen and poured himself another cup of coffee.

"Is something wrong, Mr. Monroe?"

He turned toward the table to watch Abby Andrews spoon some kind of watery cereal into her baby's mouth. One overheated van and his house had turned into a nursery overnight, and he had only Ty to thank. "That nephew of mine," he said.

"He's a sweet young man," Abby stated. "You must be proud of him."

"He thinks he's in love."

"Thinks?"

Jed shrugged. "He's young."

"I didn't know there was an age requirement."

It was said softly, but her point was made. Jed leaned against the counter and drank his coffee.

"Maybe there should be."

He watched as she efficiently wiped the baby's face with a washcloth and gave her the rest of a bottle. "Weren't you ever in love when you were—how old is Ty?"

"Nineteen," he supplied.

"Weren't you in love when you were nineteen?"

"Who wasn't?" He didn't know why he stood here talking like this. "But I don't know if you'd call it love."

"Then what would you call it?"

A constant state of arousal. "A bad case of misjudgment."

"And you don't want Ty making the same kind of mistake."

"That's right."

"You can't stop people from making mistakes. I was twenty-four when I got married."

"And you're not married anymore."

She looked pained. "No. All I'm saying is that there aren't any guarantees, no matter what your age." The baby tossed her empty bottle on the floor, and Mrs. Andrews leaned over to pick it up. She placed it on the table and then stood to lift the little girl out of the high chair.

"How old is she?"

"Thirteen months."

"You can't have been divorced very long," he said.

The baby rested comfortably on her mother's hip and wrapped her arms around her neck. "My husband walked out after I told him I was pregnant. He was thirty-four at the time, old enough to know better."

"I'm sorry." Jed sure didn't know what else to say. Where he came from, a man didn't leave his pregnant wife and two kids. But Abby Andrews's past was none of his business. He had work to do. Plenty of work, as a matter of fact. He didn't know why he was standing in the kitchen drinking coffee when he should be outside.

"I'm sorry, too. The children are going to miss having a father, but he wasn't around all that much to begin with." She shrugged and set the baby bottle in the sink. "What about Ty's girl? Is she nice?"

He put his empty mug on the counter. "What's that got to do with anything?"

"Don't you want to know what kind of a girl she is?"

"I know that already."

Abby gave him a long look. "And you don't approve. Why not? He seems like such a steady young man."

"I don't know why I'm talking about this."

"I suppose because you came in here looking like you could use a friend."

A friend? With a tempting little body and the

largest pair of gray eyes he'd ever seen? "I'd better get to work before the day's half gone."

He didn't need a friend, he told himself. And he didn't need a woman. Being alone was just fine. Hell, he *liked* it that way. Then why was he wishing that Mrs. Andrews would keep talking to him? And why was he thinking about more than conversation?

5

OKAY, so the tall rancher didn't need a friend. Abby watched him leave the kitchen, then turned to Chrissie. "He's a strange man, honey," she told the baby, who babbled her approval.

The screen door slammed again, and Abby turned to see her boss stride through the kitchen.

"Forgot something," he said as he disappeared down the hall. Abby had no sooner put Chrissie in her playpen, stationed awkwardly between the television and the saddles, when Mr. Monroe returned.

"No reason to scare the kids," he said. And then she noticed that the dark blanket over his shoulder was actually the bearskin rug.

"You don't have to do that," she assured him. "We're not here to change your house."

He paused to look down at her. "Lady, I'd appreciate a decent night's sleep tonight."

"I'm really sorry about that." She wished he wasn't quite so tall. He towered over her by at least a foot. "How tall are you?"

"Six-three. Why?"

"I just wondered."

He frowned. "And I weigh one-seventy and I have all my own teeth."

"Congratulations."

"Anything else you want to know, Mrs. Andrews?"

She caught a whiff of that rug and was glad it was leaving the house. "Actually there is." He waited, barely disguising his impatience to be gone. "Is there anything in the freezer besides pot roast?"

"I don't think so."

"Where exactly *is* the freezer?"

He hesitated. "You want me to show you now?"

Of course she did. How else was she going to earn her wages? "You can get rid of the bear first, if you want."

"Thanks."

She didn't think he was being sarcastic, because he patted the baby's head as he went past the playpen. He returned before she'd had time to finish unloading the dishwasher.

"Come on," he said, holding open the door.

"Outside?"

"Yes, ma'am. That's where the freezers are."

Abby lifted Chrissie into her arms. "Okay, lead the way."

The man paused when they were outside on the porch. "She looks heavy."

"She is, but I'm used to it."

"You want me to take her?"

From the look of fear on his face Abby knew he wanted no such thing. "Thanks, but we're fine."

"Come on, then." He led her around the corner

to a storage room attached to the corner of the house. Inside were two chest freezers, a supply of firewood and a lot of shelves lined with dusty glass jars. "My mother used to can," he explained.

Abby sincerely hoped that wasn't part of her job description, but she didn't dare ask. She wouldn't mention it if he didn't. "What's in the freezers?"

He lifted the lid of the one and bent over to look. Abby peered over his shoulder. Bulky packages wrapped in white paper lined the bottom of the freezer. Something was scrawled in black across the paper.

"Chuck roast," he read, fumbling through them. "I guess that's it. Oh, wait, here's some ground chuck."

"Hamburger?"

"There's just one package left, I guess. You want it?"

"I suppose. You don't expect me to kill any chickens, do you?"

He shut the freezer and looked at her. "Why would you think that?"

She couldn't hide her relief, especially since she had never killed anything larger than a spider. "Oh, just something Toby said."

"If you want to cook chicken, get one of the men to wring their necks for you. Otherwise just feed them and get the eggs." He opened another freezer and motioned for her to look inside.

"Now here's some vegetables, stuff like that. Old Walt was big on buying in bulk."

"We probably don't need to eat chicken," she managed to say. "Not with all that meat." She eyed the plastic bags, though they were covered in frost and the contents couldn't be seen. "Where did Walt shop?"

"In Carson." He shut the freezer door. "That's about it for the tour. Is there anything else you need?"

She could think of twenty or thirty things, but she shook her head. "Not right now."

He looked at his watch. "I'd better get moving."

"Me, too." She planned to scrub the kitchen until it gleamed and then cook a supper that would make this man glad he had hired her.

"All right then." He glanced at the baby, whose head rested on Abby's shoulder. "Is she always this quiet?"

"She's tired." She patted Chrissie's delicate back. "But I think she's glad to stop traveling for a while."

"The other kids are still asleep?"

"Yes, but I should go check on them. What time is it?"

"Almost seven."

"They'll be awake soon." She followed him out of the storage room and into the bright sunshine. "I'd better get back in."

He handed her the package of hamburger.

"You found the pantry at the north end of the kitchen?"

"Not yet."

"There's more supplies in there. If you need anything, make a list and someone will go to town on Saturday."

"Thank you."

He tipped his hat, which Abby thought was a particularly nice Western gesture, and then headed toward the largest group of outbuildings. Abby walked along the wide wooden boards that formed the porch floor and went inside the kitchen. She had a job to do, and she was about to earn her salary. She would give Mr. Jed Monroe no reason to believe he'd made a mistake in hiring a stranger.

"I COULD GET USED to this," Ty muttered. He helped himself to a big scoop of mashed potatoes and passed the bowl to his uncle.

Jed's portion wasn't any smaller than his nephew's, and he eyed the amount of food on his plate with mixed feelings. Mrs. Andrews had made meatloaf with ketchup baked on top. And mashed potatoes as creamy as his grandmother's. There were bowls of green beans and a platter of hot biscuits, though the jelly that accompanied them was store-bought. There was nothing to complain about, but Jed wished he could think of something. Not that he would have said anything out loud, he told himself, but he sure would like a reason to dislike something about the lady.

Toby and Bull were cleaner than he'd seen them since this morning, although Ty looked as if he'd been worked pretty damn hard all day. Maybe the boy would stay home tonight and sleep in his own bed.

"Is everything okay?"

She wore an apron over denim shorts again, he noticed. Her cheeks were flushed from the heat of the stove, and her hair was pulled back from her face. He tried to remember that she was a mother, but it wasn't easy unless he stopped looking at Abby Andrews's legs and started paying attention to her three kids. The baby sat in a high chair beside her brother and seemed happy to paint her face with mashed potatoes while everyone else ignored her. The two older kids ate their supper and listened to Bull's story of hunting grizzly bears.

"It was the summer of seventy-two," the old cowboy declared. "And for some reason Yellowstone couldn't hold all those bears, dunno why, but they come lookin' for food, you know, and since we were running a few hundred head up in the mountain that summer, you can believe those damn, uh, darn bears were figurin' that they were just like in a diner, picking out what they wanted and eating it right up. Just like you are."

Matt and Cass looked down at their plates, then back at the cowboy.

"How big is a grizzly bear?" Matt asked, while Cass eyed Jed.

"Mr. Monroe," she said in a shy voice, "where did your bear go?"

"He left," Jed assured her. "He's far away, out in one of the bunkhouses."

She stared at him with her mother's large gray eyes. "He can't come back to your house?"

"No."

Abby, content that her meal was being enjoyed, sat at the end of the table by her children and fixed a plate of food for herself. "I told you, Cass, Mr. Monroe took the bear out of the house this morning."

Ty chuckled. "So that's what was missing. I couldn't figure out what was different about the living room, except that it was cleaner."

Jed glared at him. "It gave the little girl nightmares."

Bull gave Abby a horrified look. "I won't tell any more grizzly stories, ma'am."

Abby smiled. "I think that would be a very good idea, Mr. Bull. At least until Cass gets used to things around here."

Jed figured it was going to be all too easy for everyone to get used to things around here, like decent meals and a clean table. Ten years was a long time for a house to be without a woman's touch, but he preferred a bachelor life-style. No offense to the pretty Mrs. Andrews, of course, but that's just the way things were. Jed tasted the meatloaf, something so tender and spicy that it didn't taste like any meatloaf Walt had tossed on the table. The biscuits were light and fluffy on the inside and crunchy on the outside.

"Is everything all right, Mr. Monroe?" Abby studied him with a grave expression.

Jed couldn't talk with his mouth full, so he nodded.

"Good," she said, smiling a little. "I found some recipes in a cabinet above the stove, so I thought I'd try some of them."

He nodded and swallowed.

"I didn't get much cleaning done," she continued, "but it took me a while to get this kitchen in shape. I had to put the saddles on the porch while I washed the floor. I hope you don't mind."

"No," he managed to say. He glanced over at the other men, who wore identical expressions of rapture as they cleaned their plates. "I'll put them in the shed so they won't be in your way."

"Would anyone like seconds?" Abby lifted the meat platter.

Of course they all did, so everything was passed around the table until the food was gone. Then the woman cleared the table before she served coffee and thick squares of spice cake topped with powdered sugar. She even gave them clean forks and plates for their dessert.

Ty had the nerve to wink, but Jed ignored him. This woman, with her tanned legs and soft voice and moist cake, couldn't be real. What did they know about her, anyway, aside from the fact that she said she was divorced and on her way to Spokane? "Mrs. Andrews," Jed began. "Where did you learn to cook like that?"

She shrugged. "Anyone who can read can cook."

"Guess Old Walt couldn't read," Bull cackled, and Toby joined in, then asked for another piece of cake. Pretty soon the cake was gone, too, though Jed noticed that chunks of it were in the baby's hair.

He tried again. "So, where did you say you were from?"

"Michigan. Outside of Detroit."

"We had a pool," Matt said. "With a diving board."

"And a great big house," Cass added, not to be outdone by her brother.

"More coffee?" Abby brought the pot over to the table and refilled their cups.

"My dad is a lawyer," Matt said. "He worked a lot."

"He had a red car," said Cass.

"Go wash your hands," their mother said, still standing by the table. "You two are excused."

"But Mom—"

"Now," she said, and the two children left the table. Abby turned to the men. "If there's nothing else I can get for you, I believe I'll start cleaning up."

"Thanks for supper," Ty said. "I don't know when I've had a better meal, not even in town."

The rest of the men murmured their thanks and lingered over their coffee. Jed pretended to listen to the conversation about tomorrow's weather and the price of hay, but he was really wondering how a woman who was married to a lawyer and had a house with a swimming pool ended up working for three hundred dollars a week in Wyoming.

"It's just not right," he told Ty later. They leaned against the corral fence and watched the sunset. "A woman like that doesn't belong here. It just doesn't make any sense."

Ty yawned. "You're looking a gift horse in the mouth."

Jed frowned. "You sure that van of hers can't be fixed?"

"I didn't say it. Bull did, and he knows a lot more about these things than we do."

"True." He tipped his hat back off his forehead. "I don't get it. How'd she go from a lawyer husband and a big house with a pool to being poor?"

"I don't know. Ask her."

"I can't ask her."

"Sure you can. Get to know her," Ty suggested. "Talk to her a little. Women like being talked to."

"And you're the expert?"

"Hey." His nephew grinned. "I'm the one with a girlfriend, not you."

"Guess I can't argue with you there."

"Don't you ever think about getting married?"

"No."

"Why not?"

"Well, for one thing we're not exactly swimming in single women around here."

The two men were quiet for a few minutes. Finally Jed broke the silence. "She said she was divorced. Said her husband walked out on her."

"She told you that?"

"Yeah. This morning. She sounded cheerful about it, too, so I guess she doesn't miss him too much."

Ty nodded. "She's probably real glad to be rid of him, so glad that she piled all her stuff in that van and left Michigan for good."

"She said she'd stay the summer. I told her she could have one of the bunkhouses, so tomorrow you can start cleaning up the big one for her."

"Which one would that be?"

"That one. With the blue door." Jed pointed in the general direction. "Didn't that used to be where the foreman lived?"

"We haven't had a foreman in forty years, Ty."

"Oh. You think the place is good enough for Abby and the kids?"

"I don't know why not. I was in there six months ago and it looked solid. Two rooms upstairs, two rooms downstairs and a bathroom. I don't know what more she'd want, and a woman needs her privacy." Especially if she's going to walk around wearing nothing but a thin nightshirt. And Jed wasn't anxious to repeat the experience of holding a rifle and standing in her bedroom door while he wore nothing but his underwear. Everyone would be better off if the woman was three hundred yards away, and under her own roof.

"She might feel safer in the main house," Ty noted pointedly. "Being a city woman and all."

"I promised her a house, and that's what she's going to get," Jed said, turning to watch the lighted windows of his home. He didn't know how many years it had been since the upstairs lights had been lit, but it sure made the house look alive again. Ty yawned as Jed turned back to him with one final order. "And you're staying home tonight, son. You can't get in trouble in your own bed."

The hell he couldn't. Ty waited for Jed to go inside the barn before he slipped across the yard to the foreman's house. He'd gotten in lots of trouble in that bed, but it was trouble of the best kind, Ty figured. And his uncle never needed to know about what happened when he'd gone to that cattle ranchers' meeting in Sheridan six weeks ago. The bunkhouse door swung open easily, because he'd oiled the hinges last weekend. He slipped inside, but didn't turn the light on. There was still enough light left to see his way around, and, satisfied that everything was the way he had left it, Ty allowed himself to dream of the future.

THIS TIME the screams only surprised him long enough to realize what was going on. Cass, the little girl with the big imagination, was certain there was a monster bull in her room and was hollering for help. Jed left the rifle on the wall and remembered to pull on his pants before running up the stairs.

He didn't stop to wonder why he felt like he should be there, but when he rounded the corner into the lit bedroom Abby smiled at him as if she was glad to have the help.

"She's dreaming she's riding a bull," she explained. "I think Mr. Bull's story last night was a little too exciting."

"He tells a lot of stories, Cass," Jed said as the little girl stared at him. She clung to her mother and eyed the intruder with huge eyes. "That doesn't mean they're true."

"He rode a bull," she whispered, glancing over at her sleeping brother to see if he was listening.

"Yes. Lots of rodeo riders do. But little girls don't." He hoped that would appease her, but she didn't look as if she believed him.

Abby added, "That's true. Children aren't allowed to ride bulls."

"Do *you* have bulls?"

"Yes, but they live far away on the other side of the ranch," he assured her.

"They do?" She yawned.

"Far away, and besides, they're not the kind of bulls that anyone rides because they're too lazy." He stepped closer to the bed without realizing what he was doing. "We had a bull named Sal once. Only he was so short that we couldn't find him half the time. He'd disappear behind trees, and Ty figured he was just hiding because he was afraid of the cows."

Cass giggled, which pleased him immensely.

He tried not to look at her mother, who would

be wearing that nightshirt again. He felt more than a little foolish. He should have stayed downstairs. Cass left her mother's arms and snuggled into her pillow.

"Thank you for helping," Abby said to him after she tucked the child's covers around her. "I'm sorry we woke you again."

"No problem." He backed out of the room and kept his eyes on her face. He didn't dare look lower. "Ty's going to clean up a place for you tomorrow."

Jed took his time going back to bed. He stopped in the kitchen for a drink of water and watched the moonlight pour through the open windows. He didn't know why he felt so damn lonely, but he sure didn't like the feeling.

He heard light footsteps in the hall, turned to see Abby enter the kitchen. She hesitated when she saw him by the window and he noticed she wore a long white robe over her nightshirt.

"Oh, excuse me, I didn't know—"

"That anyone else was awake?" he finished for her. "I was watching the full moon." He motioned toward the window. "Have you seen it?"

She stepped closer to see. He was certain she was only being polite. "It's beautiful." And then she looked at him and those gray eyes of hers looked sad. "I guess our being here is keeping you awake at night."

"Would you like a drink?"

"I came down for milk. I thought it would help me sleep."

"I need something stronger." He bent to open the cabinet below the sink. "You haven't moved the liquor, have you?"

"Not yet."

Jed found the bottle, while Abby took two stubby glasses from a cupboard. "Scotch or orange juice, Mrs. Andrews?"

"Scotch, Mr. Monroe."

He noticed her smile when he put the bottle on the counter. "What's funny?"

"You can call me Abby."

"If you will call me Jed." He poured an inch of amber liquid into each glass and set the bottle aside.

"I will," she promised, picking up her glass and touching it to his. "To no more nightmares," she said, her words soft and somehow soothing.

"To no more nightmares," he echoed, then took a hefty swallow of smoky Scotch as she sipped hers.

"Nice," was all she said as she leaned against the counter. He didn't know if she meant the drink or the moon. He knew she wasn't talking about the company. "I guess Walt didn't wake you up in the middle of the night."

"No, but he couldn't cook as well as you do, either," Jed admitted, glancing out the window again. "Your mashed potatoes are worth hearing a few screams." Abby was a foot away from him, and yet he swore he could feel the warmth radiating from her skin. He was moonstruck. Or sleep walking. He couldn't remember ever drinking

Scotch and watching the moon with a woman at three in the morning. He wanted to move away from all that tempting heat, but his feet stayed rooted to the floor.

"You Western men are easy to please."

If she only knew how easy, Jed thought. She could feed us canned beans and peanut butter and wait for the compliments that were sure to come. As long as she smiled and talked to us, we would all be content.

Abby took another sip of her drink. "I really appreciate you taking us in the way you did. I won't give you any reason to regret it."

He already did. He wanted nothing more than to touch that soft-looking triangle of bare skin that peeked above the collar of her robe. He wanted to see if she was as warm and silky as she looked, here in the moonlight, here in his kitchen. He cleared his throat and glanced toward the moon again. "Yeah, well, I guess it all worked out for the best. You have any idea what you're going to do with your rig?"

"Oh, you mean the van?"

He nodded.

"I don't know yet. I might see if it can be fixed. At least I'll find out how much it will cost and then I can go from there."

He nodded again, though he hadn't any idea what she'd said. *Fixed*, he'd heard. She must mean that piece of crap parked in the yard was going to be repaired. "Yeah," he said, forcing his big feet to move sideways, away from this woman who would be leaving as soon as she could afford to leave. He had no business thinking about her skin. He wanted no woman in his life, he reminded himself. But his body wasn't listening.

"One of these days," she said, setting down her empty glass. "I guess I can sleep now." She gave him a quick smile. "Thanks for the drink."

"Any time." That was all he could think of to say as he watched her leave the dark kitchen.

He went back to bed lonelier than he had ever been in his life. And the sheets were cold.

6

"RATS," Ty told Jed the next morning, raising his voice a little to make sure that Abby heard him over the sound of frying bacon. "*Big* ones."

Jed frowned. "We've never had rats around here. You sure what you saw wasn't a big mouse?"

"I'm sure." Ty shivered. "I wouldn't want kids living in there right now. Would you?"

"Set some traps," his uncle said. "Put out some poison. If there are rats around, they're not going to be here long."

Abby came over to the table with the coffeepot. "Are you really talking about *rats?*"

Bingo. Ty tried to keep a straight face. "In the foreman's house, Abby. So I guess you won't be able to move in right away."

She looked so disappointed that Ty felt a stab of guilt. "That's okay," she said. "We're fine upstairs for now, and I don't want the children around rats. Don't they bite?"

"We've never had this problem before," Jed said. "Maybe I should get out there and see for myself."

"I'll take care of it." Ty rushed to assure him. "You don't have to worry about a thing."

Jed continued to frown. "I sure don't understand this."

Abby hesitated at the head of the table. "I'm sorry we're keeping you awake at night, that's all."

"No problem," he told her, and then gave Ty a stern look. "See that this is taken care of."

"Sure," he agreed. "Right after breakfast." Except that once he'd killed all those imaginary rats, he'd have to think of something else. Like rusty water pipes, or faulty wiring. With any luck he could keep Abby here in the house with Jed while he worked on his own place. Ty hid a smile. Now he had an excuse to work in the house openly, and with Uncle Jed's approval, too. Finding Abby on the road that day had been a piece of luck, all right.

He couldn't wait to tell Trish, so he called her as soon as Jed left the house and Abby went upstairs with the baby.

"That isn't nice," his adored soon-to-be-bride said. "How could you scare anyone with rats?"

"There aren't really any rats," Ty explained, wondering where he'd gone wrong in explaining all of this good luck. "I just *pretended* I saw them, honey."

Silence. "That's the problem, Ty. You shouldn't have tried to scare that lady and her kids."

"But—"

"It's not nice."

He thought of his future home. And bedroom. And he couldn't feel one stab of guilt. "No, I guess you're right," he said, hoping he sounded as if he really felt bad.

"So what are you going to do?"

Now it was his turn to be silent. He stared down at his scruffy boots as if they had the answer to how to deal with women. "I'll tell her I killed all the rats, okay?"

"Okay. You won't frighten her again?"

"Not with rats," Ty promised.

Her voice brightened. "I missed you yesterday."

"Me, too. I couldn't get away. You feeling all right?"

"Sure."

"Good." They listened to each other breathe for a few moments, until Abby and her three kids entered the kitchen. "I have to go."

"Are you coming over tonight?"

"I'll try."

"I love you."

Ty darted a look at Abby, who didn't look like she was paying any attention to his conversation. Her daughter—the older one—stared up at him. "Yeah," he managed to reply. "Same here."

He hung up the phone and looked down at Cass. "Hey, kid."

"Hi, Ty." She grinned and followed him to the kitchen table. "That's a poem. *Hi, Ty.*"

"Sure is," he agreed, taking a seat across from her. "Hey, I heard you had another bad dream last night."

She nodded. "About really big bulls. I don't like them."

"Then it's a good thing they don't live around here."

Cass put her elbows on the table and rested her chin in her hands. "Mr. Monroe said they live far away."

Her older brother brought his bowl of cereal to the table and sat beside Ty. "Yeah. He told you about a billion times."

"You were sleeping."

"Yeah. Till you started screaming." He looked at Ty and rolled his eyes.

"That's enough," Abby said, putting a bowl of cereal in front of Cass. "She doesn't do it on purpose to annoy you."

"Can I have my own room?"

"No." She turned to Ty. "Would you like some more coffee? The muffins will be ready in about ten minutes."

"No, thanks, Abby." He stood and stretched. "I have to get to work or Jed will have my hide. If I don't get rid of those—"

"Don't say it!" Abby tilted her head toward Cass. "We wouldn't want to give anyone any ideas, would we?"

"Heck, no." He couldn't help feeling a little bit guilty. "Sorry about that."

Abby smiled, which made him feel even worse, since she didn't know what he was apologizing for. She was a nice lady, and she and her kids deserved a home. He grabbed his hat and jammed it on his head. All he had to do was make sure that Abby stayed here in the main house, close to Uncle Jed, and that Trish moved into the foreman's home.

With her husband.

"I'LL BE GLAD to kill a couple of chickens for you, Miz Abby," Toby offered. "Wouldn't take more'n a few minutes and we could have fried chicken for supper. Now that makes my mouth water just thinking about it. I'll bet you make great fried chicken."

Abby eyed the pen through the window and watched the fat brown hens peck in the dirt for the kernels of corn. The children loved tossing grain into the pen and watching the hens rush to find something to eat. Even Chrissie clapped her hands when the hens flapped their wings and hurried toward food.

"Maybe tomorrow," she hedged, unable to picture baking one of the children's feathered friends in a casserole dish.

"Sure." The man tipped his hat. "You just let me know and I'll fix you up with some hens real quick. Do you make cornbread?"

"Yes."

Toby grinned. "I thought you did." He bent and took Cass's hand. "Come on, young lady. I promised you and that brother of yours that you could visit the horses this afternoon, didn't I?"

Cass nodded. "Yes, Mr. Toby, you did."

Abby scooped the baby into her arms and

started toward the shady porch when she saw Ty coming out of the little house with the blue door. The foreman's house, the men called it. She decided not to get too close, just in case Ty hadn't killed all of the rats this morning.

She noticed his face was red when she came closer to him. "You should be more careful in this heat," she told him.

"I'm fine." He wiped his face on his sleeve. "Rat killing is hard business."

"I can see that," she said, noting flecks of white on his clothes. "You should be more careful with the poison."

"Huh?"

"It's all over your shirt."

"Oh." His face became even redder. "I got them all killed," he promised. "But you might want to wait a few days till you move in, just to make sure."

"I think that's a good idea," she agreed, but remembering how comfortable she felt with his uncle last night, she really didn't think living under the same roof with Jed Monroe was a good idea at all.

IT WAS A LONG WEEK. For five days Abby had planned meals, peeled potatoes, washed dishes, brewed coffee and, when she wasn't cooking, cleaned the large house. Then, in her spare time, she changed diapers, entertained the children and washed clothes. There wasn't much time left to contemplate her future or add up her money, though once in a while she did attempt to figure out how many weeks it would take before she could afford to fix her van and move on.

She had decided she couldn't bear the thought of selling it, not when it was her last connection to her former life. She'd left everything else behind, including the man she had thought she'd love forever. She'd sold the wedding gifts and the silver, the furniture and the appliances. She'd kept two boxes of Christmas ornaments, a box or two of clothes, and a couple of her favorite cookbooks, including the Cephalon skillet. There was no sense giving up everything. The husband, the house and the life-style had been enough.

No, Abby thought, today she would spend the quiet hours of the afternoon on her own finances. She would sit and think. The children had grown accustomed to "quiet time"—those hours between one-thirty and four o'clock each day when Abby concentrated on chores that got accomplished faster without children underfoot.

Abby tiptoed down the stairs so Chrissie wouldn't wake. The child had fallen asleep almost immediately after being placed in the playpen upstairs. Cass was busy with her dolls and Matt had found a book about gunfighters in Mr. Monroe's library. She didn't think he could understand most of the text, but he seemed content to study the photographs.

She took a pencil and pad to the kitchen table and sat with her checkbook and traveler's checks to add up her assets. That process didn't take long, especially without adding the van into the "plus" column.

Tomorrow, Saturday, would be her first chance to go to town. Abby turned the page of the pad and started making a list of things to do in town. First she would find a mechanic. Then she would get groceries and open a bank account so she would be able to cash her paychecks. Not that she was going to spend any money here in Wyoming, but she'd learned that life had lots of ways to disrupt the most organized plans. And she'd need a map to town, too, so she didn't end up in Nebraska instead of Carson.

She was still pondering when Jed, the man who rarely smiled, entered the kitchen and poured himself a glass of water from the kitchen faucet.

"Oh, good," she said, turning to face him. "I want to ask you about the meals."

"They're fine," he replied, and then frowned. "No one's been complaining, have they?"

"Oh, no. But I'm sure everyone's getting a little tired of beef, so I thought I'd go to town tomorrow and get groceries. How exactly do you want me to do that? Do you have a food budget?"

He shrugged. "It's just whatever we need, that's all. Some months are cheaper than other months. I can give you a check or cash. What do you want?"

"Well, I don't know. I thought I'd get more flour, sugar, yeast..." She flipped the paper to reveal her list. "Chicken, maybe a nice big turkey—if they're on sale, of course—"

"You don't have to read me the list. Just get what you think we need. And there are plenty of chickens out back. The boys will kill them and pluck them for you, if you're squeamish."

"Squeamish" was an understatement. She couldn't kill anything she fed each day. The kids had given some of them names, for heaven's sake. "If you kill them, we won't have fresh eggs." There. That sounded logical, like something a ranch woman would say. She waited for Mr. Monroe to agree with such wisdom.

"When they stop laying they turn into Sunday dinner. Seems to me that there are a few who should end up in the stew pot," he declared, then finished his water. "It's getting hot out there," he said, wiping his forehead on his sleeve. "Better tell the kids to play in the shade or they'll get heatstroke." He glanced past her toward the end of the room. "Where are they?"

"Upstairs. It's quiet time."

"For whom?" He smiled, or she thought he did. She couldn't be certain. Abby yawned, though she tried to hide it by looking down at her grocery list.

She ignored the question. "What car should I take?"

"There's the Suburban. That should hold you and the kids and the food, I guess. Can you drive a standard?"

"No." She'd never learned to change gears or use a clutch.

"I'll take you then. I've got errands, anyway, and I'll teach you how to shift on the way."

"None of the trucks are automatic?"

"Just one, but you wouldn't have room for the kids."

And there was no one to watch them here at the ranch, not that she would ever ask. These men, though kind-natured, were not what she would call nanny material. "You don't mind?"

He poured himself another glass of water and drank half of it before speaking again. "No sense both of us going in and taking two vehicles when we could use one. Besides, you'll have to learn to drive the Chevy sooner or later. Might as well be sooner, don't you think?"

Abby yawned again. She was tired of thinking. And maybe she was too old to learn new tricks like gearshifts and chicken plucking and what to do with a saddle in the living room. "Sure" was all she could come up with in response. She turned back to her list, wishing she could rest her head on the table and close her eyes. "I have a few more questions for you, Mr. Monroe, I mean, Jed."

"This going to take long?" He looked at the clock above the stove. "I've got someone due any minute."

Abby studied her list of concerns. "You'll let me know when the rats are gone?" She couldn't continue to disturb her boss with Cass's nightmares. She refused to think about the comfortable intimacy of that night, when they drank Scotch and watched the moon. She'd almost forgotten he was her boss, almost forgotten she was thirty-four and too old for romantic notions. "And did you move the gun to a safe place?"

"Yes, to both questions. Anything else?"

"Well, I thought you would want to see the grocery list," she began, but he interrupted her and raised his hand as if to ward off the evils of shopping.

"Go to bed, Abby," he said. "You look half dead and supper is five hours away. You've got time to rest."

"I don't—" Her own yawn stopped her again, but her boss didn't notice. The man was already across the kitchen and out the door. She stared at the floor, noticing he'd tracked footprints of dirt across the linoleum. She turned back to her list and wrote *mat for the kitchen door.*

HE COULD HAVE GOTTEN a drink at the bunkhouse. Or at the faucet outside the barn. He kept some plastic jugs in the back of his truck, too, for emergencies. He didn't need to walk into the kitchen for water and it disgusted him to think he'd done it just so he could get a glimpse of Abby.

Jed knew he was no better off than the others, who started getting happy and anxious when it was close to dinnertime. 'Course, the rest of the men were too old for her. Unless she preferred older men. And Ty was too young. Unless she preferred younger men.

No, she didn't seem to prefer men at all. At

least not right now. He didn't think someone who had just divorced a fancy lawyer would be looking around for another man in her life. Especially one who smelled more like cow than aftershave.

Jed ran his hand over his rough cheek. He should shave before supper. Shower, too. Then he frowned. He wasn't looking for a woman. Those days were over. He'd wear his sweat-stained shirt and he'd wait to shave in the morning, just as he always did.

No pretty little woman was going to make him change his ways. She'd be gone as soon as she could afford to buy the rig that would take her west. And he'd be here, same as always. Alone.

Friday night was the same as any other night on the Gem, except that Ty put on a fancy shirt and didn't sit down with the rest of them for dinner. Abby, fresh from a nap, thought he looked very handsome. And very young.

"I've got a date," he boasted, his hair damp and slicked back from a recent shower.

Jed looked up from his plate piled with pot roast stew. "Where are you off to?"

"We're going to town to see a movie."

No one asked what he was going to see except Matt, who preferred action films. "*Lethal Weapon 4?*"

"Dunno," the young man said. "Whatever's in town, that's what we'll see."

Matt's jaw dropped. "You only have one movie?"

"Excuse my son," Abby said, setting another

basket of hot biscuits on the table. "He comes from the Land of the Suburbs."

The five men gave the boy sympathetic looks.

"No wonder you don't have a nickname," Bull declared. "Can't have a nickname when you grow up in town."

"You can't?"

"Nope." Bull winked. "You come with me after supper and we'll go find ourselves something to do that just might give you a name fer yourself."

"Cool," said her son, digging his fork into a chunk of potato. "I'm sick of playing with Cass all the time. Are we gonna ride bulls?"

"Hell, I mean heck, son. You've only sat on a horse twice in yer whole life. What makes you think you'd be riding bulls?"

Matt grinned and shot a look at his sister. "I was just kidding. I wanted to hear Cassandra Louise scream."

Cass did, much to Abby's dismay. "Shush," she told her daughter. "That's enough out of you." She sat down across from the children, next to the high chair where Chrissie smeared potatoes on the tray.

"Tomorrow's still a workday," Jed reminded his nephew, who winked at Matt.

"Yep, Uncle Jed, I know. How many years have I been working for you?" He reached over and helped himself to a biscuit.

"Eleven or twelve."

"Long enough to know that Saturday's a workday." He finished the biscuit on his way out the door. "These are great, Abby. Guess everyone should thank me for bringing you home last week."

"Yeah, kid," Toby drawled. "You're smarter than you look."

"Be careful," Jed called after him, just as the screen door bounced shut. "The kid thinks he's in love," he said to the group gathered around the table.

Silence greeted that pronouncement.

Abby lifted the casserole dish. "Would anyone care for more stew?"

"Me, me, me," chanted the baby, and a splash of tomato sauce flew across the table and landed on Jed's shoulder. He didn't seem to notice, though.

"He's too damn young," Jed continued, taking the dish from Abby and filling his plate again. "Am I the only one who thinks the boy's heading for trouble?"

Abby smiled. "Don't you remember what it was like to be young and in love?"

"Yes," the rancher replied, handing the dish back to her. "And if I had it to do over again, I would have saved myself the trouble."

"Isn't that a little, um, harsh?"

"I would think, Mrs. Andrews, that you would understand."

She felt herself flush, whether from anger or embarrassment she wasn't sure. Abby took a deep breath before she lifted her gaze to the man across the table. "I don't regret having my family." Her voice was soft. "Everything has its price."

He smiled, but those dark eyes of his didn't give away anything. "Yes, ma'am, at least we agree on that much."

7

"THIS IS FIRST GEAR," Jed explained, pointing to the diagram above the stick shift as he demonstrated how it worked. "Think of it as the letter H, with an extra hook for reverse. Don't bother with any of that other stuff, because that's four-wheel drive and you won't be needing it."

"All right." She nodded, and leaned closer. He could have done without her being closer, but he told himself it was nothing to him if Abby's shiny hair smelled like apples. "When you need to shift, just step on the clutch." He demonstrated. "Like this. Don't try to shift without using the clutch. Got that?"

"Yes." She turned to the children who bounced and giggled in the wide back seat. "Keep your seat belts on and stop teasing Chrissie."

Jed looked in the rearview mirror and caught a glimpse of the baby's smile. She didn't seem to mind the car seat at all, but that pink frilly hat on her head looked ridiculous. "Why is she wearing that?"

"What—oh, the hat? I try to keep the sun off her face whenever I can. Skin cancer, you know," Abby replied as she settled herself back in her seat and readjusted the seat belt. "Why don't we get started and you can explain to me why you're shifting."

He should have let someone else take her into Carson this morning, but Ty couldn't be trusted to stay away from the Jensen place and the other men all had work to do that couldn't wait. Since he was the only one who could do the banking and since the bank was open until noon on Saturdays, Jed really had no choice but to start the engine and shift the car into reverse. "Reverse takes a little practice," he cautioned, backing up past the trucks until the car was headed in the right direction. "Now for the clutch. I let out the clutch and step on the gas real easy, so that we move forward. In first gear."

"Okay." Abby rummaged through her purse and pulled out a notebook. "I thought we could talk about meals. Do you have anything against salads?"

He shifted to second gear as the driveway flattened out. "I'm shifting to second. Same thing. Step on the clutch, shift it into second, then release the clutch. Salads? Why would I have anything against salads?"

"Good. I'm going to start serving them at lunch and supper. Why did you shift again?"

"Speed."

"How do you know *when* to shift?"

"You can hear the engine."

"Oh." She gave him an odd look. "This is starting to sound very difficult."

"You'll get the hang of it when you drive home."

She turned back to her pad when they got onto the main road and headed south to town. He shifted twice more, until they were in fourth gear and cruising along at sixty, but Abby only nodded at his explanations of the gearshift and asked if she could buy a ham.

"I'll butcher the hog in the fall," he said, "but if you want to get a ham, go ahead."

"You haven't had one recently?"

There were a lot of things he hadn't had recently, he thought wryly, glad she couldn't read his thoughts. He concentrated on the food question instead of her eyes. He'd bought fifty pounds of bacon last year, come to think of it. "I doubt it."

"Good. I can bake one and we can use the leftovers for sandwiches." She made more notes on the pad in her lap, while Jed tried not to glance over at her every few seconds. It was real strange to be driving a woman to town. He couldn't remember ever doing it before. Old Walt had never talked about ham sandwiches or salads. He didn't remember Walt having much to say at all, unless it was about the weather.

A man could get real tired of talking about the weather.

"Are summers here really hot?" Abby asked.

"Well, yeah, I guess. Why?"

"I wondered if you wanted hot meals all the time, even on hot days. I'm working on menus for the month."

"We eat big around the Gem. Have to, with all the work there is to do. I'll put the air conditioner in the kitchen window for you soon as we get back."

"That would help."

"You're planning on staying a month, then?" He didn't stop to wonder why his heart lifted at the thought.

"At least," she murmured, flipping the pages of her notebook. "I've done the math, and today I'll talk to someone about fixing my van and see what I can afford."

Curiosity overcame his better judgment. "Lady, how did you end up divorcing a rich lawyer and not having any money?"

She shrugged. "I was too trusting. Do you know who I could talk to about fixing my van? Bull said he would do it, if he'd had the parts, but he told me that he'd have to order a rebuilt engine and that might take a while, because he could only work on it during his day off."

Meaning, Jed assumed, that Bull wanted to keep the cook around for as long as he could. There was something about whipped potatoes that got under a man's skin. "Yeah, well—"

"And I thought I'd take Toby's advice and see what other cars cost. I could always take out a loan if I could afford the down payment."

"Well, that's true, but how are you going to get a loan if you're not going to live here?" When was the last time he'd made love to a woman?

"I could lease," she mused, not answering his

question. "But I've heard that has its pitfalls, too. But it would be one way to get to Spokane without mechanical problems."

"If you can afford it," he reminded her, not liking the idea of Abby in Spokane. Jed gripped the steering wheel and stepped on the gas. What on earth was the matter with him? If he had any sense he'd loan the woman enough money for a down payment on a sensible sedan and she would be out of his life in a matter of days.

But he had no sense, no sense at all. Hell, he liked having her around the ranch. He liked her smile and he liked the way her hair smelled. Oh, he could do without the 3:00 a.m. screaming sessions and the boy's constant questions and the baby's bottles blocking the platters of beef in the fridge. He would never be a family man. He was too old. But he liked the woman. Probably because she was only temporary and he was safe from the kind of commitment that would take up too much of his time.

He was too old for broken hearts. When a man reached forty, he was safe from that nonsense. Jed glanced toward Abby one more time and didn't feel safe at all.

HIDING THE CHICKEN was easy. Not even the children, distracted by a rack of comic books, noticed what went into the shopping cart. Abby piled ham and toilet paper on top of the plastic bags stuffed with nice, anonymous, naked poultry. They had no names, they had never lived on the ranch, they had never pecked at feed tossed by her children. They would make lovely guilt-free meals for everyone on the Gem. And no one would have to know they'd come from the Super Save in Carson.

She'd bought Matt a *Star Wars* comic, Cass a coloring book, the baby a ring of plastic keys; she'd been careful to keep her purchases separate from those for the ranch. The woman behind the cash register told her to enjoy her stay in Carson. Jed had shown no patience for grocery shopping and had instead headed toward the bank across the street. He'd given her a blank check and tipped his hat before he left. He'd said he'd meet her in the parking lot.

Chrissie sat in the front of the shopping cart, her pudgy hands gripping the same metal bar that Abby held. "Go, go, go!" she cried.

"Did Matt teach you to say that?"

The baby grinned, a happy vision beneath the lace-trimmed hat. Abby paused to retie the bow under Chrissie's damp chin. "Let's go find our ride," she told the children beside her.

Matt hesitated. "Do we hafta go back now?"

Abby paused in the shade of Super Save's roof until she spotted Jed's Suburban. "Come on," she urged the children. "I see him."

"Can we walk around?" her son urged her again. "I'm hungry."

"We'll eat when we get home," she promised. "I only have to make one more stop."

"Where?" Cass asked, hanging on to the cart as they crossed the parking lot.

"To look at cars."

Matt perked up. "We getting a new one?"

"I *like* the van," her daughter said. "Can't we keep it?"

"I don't know," she told them. "I have to figure it out."

"We could go back home," Matt said, his eyes huge and suspiciously bright. "We could ask Dad for a new car."

Abby stopped the cart a few feet away from her destination and knelt to look at Matt. "Honey, we can't. Your father loves you—" she wanted to choke on the words, but she managed what she hoped was a convincing expression "—but he is very busy with work. And we don't have the house anymore, remember?"

"But I miss my friends."

"I know, but you'll make new ones in Spokane." She straightened when she saw Jed approach. "I promise. And you can write to all of your friends back home and tell them you lived on a real ranch this summer."

Matt's face brightened. "Cool."

"*Way* cool," his sister agreed, peeking into an overflowing grocery bag. "Look. Mom bought Oreos."

Jed refused her help with the groceries, and by the time she'd settled the children into the car he'd unloaded the cart and stored the bags in the back section of the car. Abby didn't mind getting out of the sun. She didn't mind waiting while someone else took charge. These Western men had their advantages, all right.

"Anything else?" Jed asked as he turned the key in the ignition.

"I'd like to talk to a car dealer. And maybe a mechanic?"

"I thought you would. I'll drive you through town and give you the tour."

Carson was larger than she had expected. Jed drove her down Main Street, past stores, a restaurant, two gas stations and a post office. Side streets held small houses with neat front lawns. There were pickup trucks everywhere and a smattering of motor homes parked along the sides of the street.

"Tourists," Jed explained. "They take the back roads once in a while and end up here." He stopped at a red light and pointed toward another street. "Up there is the elementary school and the junior high. We just built a new high school farther out of town."

"It seems like a nice place," Abby said, surprised by the number of people in town. Several men and one woman waved to Jed as he drove past. "Is it always this busy?"

"Sure. It's Saturday. It's a small town, but there are a lot of ranches in these parts. It's at least ninety miles to find a bigger town, so most people in the county do their business here."

Carson looked like a town that would have existed unchanged fifty years ago, the kind of place where generation after generation lived, never leaving their wives and children for younger female lawyers.

"Shift it into first," Jed said. "It's in neutral now, but the light just turned green."

"I don't—"

"Just do it. We're holding up traffic."

Abby scooted closer and took hold of the knob. "Forward, right?"

"Yeah. Straight up."

She couldn't do it, so Jed moved his large hand over hers and guided the stick shift into the proper position. His rough fingers enfolded hers in a surprisingly intimate way, one that made her heart stop for a foolish second or two before beating faster. His hand stayed on hers as the car moved forward, as if he had no desire to remove it. And Abby couldn't—wouldn't—protest his touch, though she kept her gaze on the road in front of them as if she, instead of the silent man beside her, was driving the Suburban.

"There," he said after many long seconds. He lifted his hand and put it on the steering wheel. "Did you feel it?"

Her skin tingled as if she was fourteen again and had just held hands with the cute boy on the school bus. "Excuse me?"

"Where first gear is. Did you feel it?"

"Yes." She took her hand away and sat back in her seat.

"Good. We'll do that a few times until you get the hang of it."

"Good idea," she managed to mumble. She was thirty-four, and just because she hadn't been touched in any way, shape or form since she gave birth to Chrissie—and hadn't had sex since the baby was conceived—didn't mean she had to overreact during a driving lesson.

She was too old for this kind of behavior. And the last thing she wanted was a man in her life, now that she was finally getting her life together again.

Ty MOVED HIS HAND to Trish's flat stomach. "No one's going to believe you're going to have a baby," he said, kissing her neck. Kissing wasn't easy on the front seat of his truck, but they'd managed before and they would manage again. At least until they could move into their own home.

She put her hand over his. "They will in a few months. Have you talked to your uncle again?"

"No, but I'll try again tomorrow."

"You're going to have to tell him about the baby, Ty. That's the only thing that's going to work."

"I know. I was just hoping I wouldn't have to." Ty closed his eyes and pictured Uncle Jed's face when he discovered his nephew had gotten a girl pregnant. He'd be lucky if he escaped the house with his manhood intact. Maybe he'd better tell him when they were both working outside, when Ty was on horseback and Uncle Jed was standing around with his hands in his pockets.

"He can't stay mad at you forever."

"Yeah, but he's gonna be just as mad as your dad's gonna be, and we need Jed's help when that hits the fan."

She snuggled into his chest. "I know. I just get scared."

He put his arms around her and held her tightly against him. "Uncle Jed's getting used to having a woman around the house," he told her. "We need him on our side, Trish, or your father will send you away. Maybe we should elope after all."

She lifted her head to look at him. "I'm not running away like there's something to be ashamed of. I'm going to have a real wedding, just like I'm going to have a real baby." With that, she burst into tears.

Ty patted her on the back and felt his shirtfront grow soggy. Maybe it was time to see how much Uncle Jed had mellowed.

HE COULDN'T SLEEP. At least not all night through. At two o'clock Sunday morning Jed gave up and, stopping to check into Ty's empty bedroom, headed for the kitchen. He told himself he was worried about Ty. He wasn't busy picturing a very desirable woman asleep in her bed upstairs. He wasn't imagining Abby curled up beside him, underneath his grandmother's quilt. No, Jed told himself, pouring a generous helping of whiskey into a glass, he was too old to be mooning over a woman who was only on his ranch to earn enough money to leave. Jed sat in the semi-darkness and waited to feel tired enough to go back to bed, but he was on his second drink before he realized he wasn't going to be alone.

He heard her footsteps before she entered the kitchen, so he took his drink over to the table as she came into the room.

Abby hesitated when she saw him. "We woke you again?"

"No. I couldn't sleep. Ty's not home yet." Which was as good an excuse as any, he supposed. He noticed she made sure her robe was tied securely. "Care to join me?"

She smiled, and his heart rolled over. "This could become a habit, you know."

Oh, he knew, all right. He watched her take a glass from the cupboard and pick up the bottle of Jack Daniel's before she joined him. She sat across from him and for the slightest moment her bare feet brushed his.

"Excuse me," she said, flushing slightly as she poured herself a drink.

"Did Cass have another nightmare?"

"No. This time it was Chrissie. She cried and woke me up. She went back to sleep, but I didn't." She held out her glass. "Here's to a good night's sleep," she said, touching her glass to his.

"Amen," he answered, glad she couldn't read his thoughts. Her hair lay tousled and silky against the collar of the robe, her cheeks were flushed and she smelled like violets. He wondered why she wore perfume to bed. Had her husband liked the scent of flowers when he made love to her? He took her hand and turned it over to expose her palm. The whiskey made him bold, bold enough to lift her hand and bring it to his nose. "Violet perfume?"

She gently tugged her hand away and cupped her glass. "Bath powder."

He closed his eyes for just a second, which was long enough to wonder if the whiskey had gone to his head. No, he was fine. Just tired, that was all.

"Why are you awake?" she asked.

"Ty's still not home."

"Are you worried?"

"A little, but I pretty much know where he is. With his girlfriend, of course."

"What do her parents say about her being out this late?"

"Her mother's dead and her father's most likely passed out at Murphy's Bar. He'll make it home in the morning after he sobers up, and Ty, if he has any sense, will be long gone by then."

"Maybe they *should* get married," she murmured. "At least you would know he was here on the ranch at night."

Jed shrugged. "He's too young. Can you picture Matt getting married ten or eleven years from now?"

"I can't even picture Matt picking up his own clothes," she admitted, taking another sip of her drink.

"Ty still doesn't do that." He leaned back in his

chair. "You didn't tell me what you found out about the car."

She winced. "I was too busy concentrating on shifting, remember?"

He remembered, all right. Why else would he still be awake, drowning his senses in alcohol? Her hand on the knob of that stick shift was an erotic image that would keep him awake for many nights to come. "How much money do you need?"

"He offered me a trade-in on the van that seemed fair. That and three thousand dollars will get me a nineteen eighty-five Cadillac with low mileage and an automatic shift."

"Was it a white Cadillac with blue interior?"

"Yes, but how—"

"Doc Adams's old car. His widow banged it up a few times, but I'll bet Carl fixed the dents."

"I didn't notice any dents." She finished her drink and poured herself another one.

"It should be a good car for you," he reassured her, "but it's a gas hog. You'd better be prepared to spend some money at every gas station between here and Washington."

"I didn't say I was going to buy it."

"True." He touched his glass to hers. "Here's to, uh, travel. And good gas mileage."

"To travel," she echoed, though she sounded doubtful.

"I could loan you the three thousand," he said. "Pay me back after you get to Spokane and get a job." He would be able to sleep again. He would be able to enter his kitchen in the morning without his body reminding him how long it had been since he'd taken a woman to bed.

"I couldn't do that," she said, her eyes dark as she looked at him. "It wouldn't be right."

"Why not?"

"I'll earn my way," she said, her mouth turning down at the corners. He wanted to touch her lips and make her smile at him. "But I appreciate the offer."

"You want to get there all by yourself," he stated. "Is that it?"

"Yes. I was married for ten years and I depended on my husband for everything. Which turned out to be a mistake. And I'm not going to do that again. Depend on anyone else, I mean."

He understood. Hell, that would keep her here on the Gem longer. He reminded himself that he shouldn't feel so relieved. He was supposed to be trying to get her out of his life, not keep her here longer. Just a little while longer. Nothing permanent, of course.

And when she reached across the table and gave his hand a squeeze, it just meant that she was saying good-night, a silent thank-you for his offer of help. He didn't mean to stand when she did, there in the soft darkness of the kitchen. He sure didn't intend to meet her at the head of the table and take her into his arms.

Her lips were warm, parted slightly as if she was surprised to be kissed. Intrigued by the tempting sweetness of her body against his, Jed realized he hadn't exactly planned for this to happen, either. But he was enjoying every second of it.

8

INSANITY was not a good thing, Abby decided, climbing back into her bed. Neither was lust. Kissing her boss at—she looked at her clock on the nightstand—2:33 in the morning was a mistake of the most serious kind. What on earth had she been thinking?

Nothing, of course. Only that it felt good to be held, that the sweet pressure of his warm and slightly chapped lips tempted her to move closer into his arms until he'd held her against that broad chest of his. It had been a satisfyingly long kiss, as if neither one of them wanted to end it. Until it seemed that they would end up sprawled on the long table, that is. And she had left him standing there.

Abby snuggled under the covers, careful not to jostle the baby who slept so peacefully in the corner. In three hours she would waken and start frying bacon. In three hours she would pour Jed his coffee and say "good morning" in a formal way that would make him understand that she didn't want to think about what had happened between them.

It was just a kiss, she reminded herself. She was too old and too busy and too darn poor to look at that man as anything but the person who signed her paycheck. No matter how rugged and sexy and interesting he appeared.

And that, she decided, was the last she'd think about it. She ran her fingers over her lips while she debated whether to have fried chicken or baked ham for supper.

JED DRANK SEVEN CUPS of coffee Sunday morning. There was so much caffeine buzzing through his brain he figured he might just explode, and all because he'd kissed Abby last night and now he was trying to apologize.

And he was going to sit here, chugging Maxwell House and picking at warm muffins until he damn well had a chance to say something to the woman. Something like how it would never happen again, which was a withering thought. He wanted to do a lot more than kiss her, especially as he watched Abby scurry around the kitchen. She had flour up to her elbows, a smudge of cinnamon on her cheeks, and when she bent over the oven to remove hot muffins, well, he'd had to shift in his seat and be grateful no one could see his obvious physical reaction to the sight of Mrs. Andrews in denim shorts.

"Ba, ba, ba," chanted the baby. She banged a spoon on the tray of her high chair, sending oatmeal chunks spraying across the table. Jed didn't mind the globs on his arm. He did notice that the saddles were no longer in the corner, flowers sat in a vase on the table, and the old linoleum gleamed like new. Well, almost new. Those worn areas by the door couldn't be scrubbed away.

"Abby," he tried again, clearing his throat. "About last—"

"You ready for more coffee?" She lifted the carafe, but didn't meet his gaze. He guessed she didn't want to talk to him. "Are you waiting for another round of muffins?"

"Coffee is fine," he said, deciding not to risk lifting his mug and letting her see him shake. "Uh, Abby, I—"

"They're hot, but you can have as many as you want." She scooted away and headed back to the safety of the stove.

"I don't want muffins," he mumbled, standing and pushing his chair back.

"Ba, ba, ba," Chrissie hollered, smacking that spoon as hard as she could. *"Ba, ba!"*

Jed hesitated. "What's she yelling about?"

"She wants a *b-o-t-t-l-e*," Abby said. "And she has to wait until I'm finished here."

Chrissie looked at him and hollered again.

"She's not the most patient little thing, is she," he muttered, not expecting an answer. Abby was busy piling hot muffins into a basket lined with a cloth. Where did she find this stuff? He kept heading in her direction, though, figuring it was now or never. "Abby, I'm sorry about last night."

There. He'd gotten it out. So it was a lie. At least he had the balls to say he was sorry. He couldn't remember ever saying those words in his life.

"Sorry?"

Jed turned to see Ty and a pretty blond girl enter the kitchen from the back porch.

Ty grinned at him as he looped his arm around the girl's neck. "Uncle Jed, that's one word you never use. What are you *sorry* about?"

"That you're not somewhere else," Jed muttered, edging away from Abby. That kid had ears like a hawk.

"Yes," said Abby, handing him a basket of muffins as if that's what he'd been waiting for. "What are you *sorry* about, Jed?"

The lady looked at him as if she dared him to mention last night, so Jed shook his head. "I guess I'm not sorry about one damn thing," he stated, staring right into Abby Andrews's gray eyes. "It's your day off, Mrs. Andrews. What are you going to do with it?"

She frowned, then her cheeks flushed pink. "I have no idea."

Ty chuckled and seated his girlfriend at the table. "I think Uncle Jed is feeling guilty, Abby. He's making you work too hard."

Guilty? Jed shot a quick look at his nephew and said hello to the Jensen girl. She'd grown up, he noted. No more gangly limbs, no more ribbons in her hair. No wonder Ty was acting like a spring bull.

"I forgot about my day off," Abby said, looking at the basket of muffins. She smiled at Ty. "You mean I could have slept late?"

"Yes, ma'am," his nephew replied. "It's everyone's day off, except we all take turns doing chores in the morning. Abby, meet Trish Jensen. My fiancée. Trish, this is Mrs. Andrews. Abby."

"Hi, Trish." Abby put the muffins on the table between the teenagers. "Have you had breakfast?"

"Yes."

"No."

"Well?" Abby chuckled. Jed could see she was pleased to have more people in the kitchen so that she could avoid him. And wouldn't have to talk to him. He wondered if she would quit now. But no, where would she go? He felt like a idiot.

"We'd love breakfast, Mrs. Andrews," the girl said, leaving her seat. "If you'll let me help."

"Okay, then. You can crack these eggs."

Jed took a few steps back, until he was close to the high chair and the baby, who was suddenly engrossed in pulling apart a magazine. Ty leaned toward his uncle. "I thought maybe you and Trish could get to know each other."

He had no idea how to reply to that statement. How was he supposed to befriend an eighteen-year-old girl?

"I think I got rid of the rats," Ty whispered, after glancing at the women who were breaking eggs into a bowl at the kitchen counter. "But there's some trouble with the roof. It's leaking."

"It hasn't rained in two weeks."

"Yeah, well, there's a water stain. And there's supposed to be rain by Wednesday," he said. "You wouldn't want the little kids to get wet, would you? The ceiling could collapse and—"

"Yeah, go ahead and do what you can. If you need a hand—"

"Trish will help me. Her dad's gone to Casper to visit his brother, so she's going to hang out with me for a while."

"I didn't know you had time to 'hang out.'"

Ty shrugged. "I just thought—"

"Ty? How do you want your eggs?" the teenager called. Cass and Matt ran in, greeted Trish, and rushed over to the television set. Jed noticed that Abby had moved that, too, along with the old couch, to a less central part of the big room. The weather channel disappeared, to be replaced by cartoons and toy commercials.

"Turn that down," their mother told the children. Then she caught Jed's eye. "I told them they could watch television for a while if they cleaned up their room, but if you want to watch the weather, then they can go somewhere else."

"Not the living room," Cass stated. "The bear could come back."

"He's gone," Jed assured her, as he did every morning. And her response was the same.

"Maybe," she would say, and give him a look as though he was hiding the damn bear and waiting to spring it on her when she least expected it.

Toby and Bull banged on the screen door, lured by the smell of baking, no doubt, and stepped into the kitchen.

"Well, well," Bull said, grinning. "Didn't know we wuz havin' a party this mornin'."

Ty introduced the love of his life to the two

cowhands, who took off their hats and waited to be invited for coffee and muffins. They knew that Abby would make them sit and eat, of course. Which she did. Jed knew he should be checking the horses, planning ahead for the hay crew, doctoring calves and checking fence, but he couldn't move.

Wouldn't move. It was Sunday, after all, and a man couldn't be expected to work eighteen hours a day, seven days a week. He got up and took his empty coffee mug over to the counter. Abby poured coffee for the men and then turned to Jed, who held out his cup.

"I'll have a little warm-up, if you don't mind," he said, figuring he'd eat four or five more muffins to sop up the acid in his stomach.

"Sure." She poured his coffee. "And if you say you're sorry about last night I'll pour this in your lap."

"I'm not sorry," he muttered, eyeing the coffeepot. "I was lying."

"Good," she said, moving away to refill other coffee cups. She shouldn't be working so hard, he thought. If she wasn't working, he'd have her all to himself.

"I SEE WHAT YOU MEAN." Trish leaned against the worn boards of the horse corral and rested her chin on her hands; Ty stood beside her. Both of them stared unseeing at the horses that meandered in the enclosure.

"So what do we do next?"

"He likes her."

"Think so?"

"Yes," Trish said, obviously sure of her female instincts. "But I don't know about *her*. That could go either way."

Ty sighed. He was lucky to be marrying such a wise woman. "So what do we do?"

"Let me think."

He put his arm around her and whispered, "The house is empty. You want to take a look at what I've done?"

"Not right now," she said, much to his disappointment. He'd already figured he could roll out that new carpet...

"You don't?" He nuzzled her neck. "We'd have the place all to ourselves for as long as we want."

Trish pulled away and turned toward him. "But what about Abby? And your uncle?"

For some reason his brain wouldn't come up with anything intelligent to say. "What *about* them?"

"We're supposed to be fixing them up," Trish reminded him. "So your uncle understands how it feels to be in love, or else he'll be so happy to have a woman of his own that he won't pay attention to us at all. And we can get *married*."

"Yeah," Ty agreed, trying not to think about Trish naked on the blue carpet. She put her arms around his waist and hugged him.

"And then we can spend all the time we want

alone in our little house and no one can tell me to go home or you to go to work."

Ty doubted that. "Jed's always gonna be telling me to go to work." And he really didn't mind all that much. After all, Uncle Jed was all the family he had. Raising a kid couldn't have been easy for an old bachelor like Jed, but he'd managed. And promised that when Ty was twenty-five and got the money from his mother's trust fund, he could buy back his father's share of the ranch and become a partner. A man couldn't get any more fair than Jed, and Ty sure didn't mind working for him. At least most of the time he didn't. "I'm not afraid of work, not when part of this is gonna be mine too, someday."

"You're not afraid of anything," Trish agreed. "That's why I love you."

Ty grinned as he tugged on Trish's hair. He liked the part about spending time together alone in their house. "We're gonna need curtains."

"Curtains?" She looked up at him and frowned. "Ty, we have to start thinking about *them*."

Yeah. Them. He wondered if they were too old to have sex, then figured they probably weren't. Maybe once a month or so, nothing too strenuous. Besides, Jed liked to go to bed early. The man needed his sleep and was a real bear to live with if he didn't get his eight or nine hours in. And Ty should know. "You have any ideas?"

She took his hand and tugged him toward the

house. "I think we should offer to baby-sit so that they can go out together."

"Baby-sit?"

"Sure. It'll be fun. And we need the practice." She squeezed his hand. "Isn't that baby the sweetest thing you've ever seen?"

"Yeah, Chrissie's cute, but I don't think Abby's going to want to go out with Jed, and he never goes out on dates."

"Today he will," she announced, and Ty let himself be led toward the house. "I think I have a plan."

Well, heck, he had a plan, too. And that plan meant getting naked in the foreman's house for an hour or two, and *then* deciding how to deal with Jed. "Hey, honey, I have a better idea."

She stopped. "You do?"

He whispered his ideas into her ear, which made her smile. "Hold that thought, Ty, honey," she told him. "We'll have time for that later. I hope."

She hoped? Ty ached with frustration. If Uncle Jed didn't fall in love soon, Ty was going to be one unhappy cowboy.

"I REALLY DON'T NEED to go anywhere," Abby explained, wiping her hands on a dish towel. "I'm going to slice this ham and everyone can make sandwiches, and the beans are ready to go into the oven, and—"

"But it's your day off," the pretty little teenager insisted. "You shouldn't be cooking."

Abby could see why Ty liked the girl so much. She was a young woman who looked as if nothing could topple her over. Braided hair, big blue eyes, no makeup—and there was quite a body packed into a pink shirt and worn denim jeans. Trish lifted Chrissie from her high chair and settled her on her hip. "Do you do a lot of babysitting?"

"Yes, I used to. Before Dad needed me to work in the kitchen." She kissed the baby's hair. "She is *so* sweet. All of your kids are so well-behaved. How do you do it all by yourself?"

"It's not easy," Abby admitted. "But I really didn't have any choice."

Trish nodded. "Your husband was a real creep, huh?"

Abby tried not to laugh. "I guess you could say that."

"You should stick around here," Trish said, for all the world as if she was thirty-four, too. "There are tons of single men, you know, who would be happy to have a wife."

"I'm not looking for a husband, Trish." She wouldn't disillusion the girl and explain that men were not to be trusted to keep their promises, or were too attracted to firm flesh and exciting affairs on business trips. She took Chrissie's bottle from a pan of hot water and wiped it dry before handing it to Trish. "I don't intend to ever marry again."

"I can feed her?"

"Sure, if you want to."

Chrissie grabbed the bottle and stuck it in her mouth, while Trish giggled. "She's awfully smart." She smiled at Abby. "I can't wait to have kids of my own."

Abby shook her head, but decided to mind her own business. Young love would have to run its course, and divorced women should keep their mouths closed. She busied herself with scrubbing the last of the breakfast frying pans.

"...And should see it, don't you think?"

"What?"

"The ranch. You should see it."

Abby rinsed the pans and stacked them on the drainboard. "I've never seen a ranch," she admitted. "This is all new to me."

Trish looked pleased. "I thought so. I'll ask Ty to give you a tour this afternoon, okay? I'd be glad to watch the kids for you for a while."

"Well, I don't know. Are you sure? The baby will sleep for at least two hours, and Matt and Cass will play in the yard. But you have to watch to make sure they don't wander off where they're not supposed to go."

"Sure I'm sure. I'd like to do that."

"Well, you make it hard to say no." Abby wiped her hands and took out a pitcher of iced tea. "Do I have to ride a horse?"

"Not if you don't want to. He can use the truck, which is lots easier, okay?"

"Okay," Abby agreed once again. "I haven't ridden a horse since I was nine."

Trish took the empty bottle from the baby. "Oh,

it's easy enough, especially with the horses around here. They're as tame as kittens."

"Somehow I doubt that."

The teenager cuddled the baby close to her. "What do you want me to do with this one?"

"I'll take her. She's late for her morning nap."

She lifted the baby from Trish's arms and held her against her shoulder. "Help yourself to iced tea."

"Maybe later. I'll go tell Ty that he's about to become a tour guide."

"He won't mind?" Somehow she doubted that the young man would enjoy being separated from his "fiancée."

"Nope. Not a bit."

Abby decided to believe her, which was her second mistake. The first was agreeing to tour the ranch in the first place. But she didn't realize that until thirty minutes later, when she stepped into a battered brown truck and saw the Monroe who was going to show her the Gem.

"I thought Ty was—"

"Matt was supposed to—"

Abby shut the door and fastened her seat belt. "I guess Ty changed his mind," she said as Jed drove the truck over a hill and away from the ranch.

"He asked me to show Matt where we used to fish."

Jed was going to take her son fishing? Abby stared in amazement.

"I think we've been set up," the rancher continued. "Those kids are determined to be alone, and they've just figured out how to do it."

"Uh-oh. They're supposed to be baby-sitting, not having...well, you know." There was no doubt in Abby's mind that those two teenagers had that "we've discovered the joys of sex" glow.

Jed glanced toward her and took his foot off the gas. "You think they're...I mean, do you think that's what they're doing?"

"I hope not." Matt and Cass didn't need to add that to their memories of What I Saw on My Summer Vacation.

"We can go back," he offered, slowing the truck to a crawl. "But if you've never seen a cattle ranch before, this might be as good a time as any. And Ty likes your kids. He'll take good care of them."

He was right. Besides, Cass wouldn't leave Trish alone long enough for anyone to get into trouble. She already wanted to braid her hair just like the teenager's. "All right," Abby said. "I'd like to see where you work."

"I keep forgetting you're a city girl."

"Not a city girl, exactly." She smiled and gripped the dashboard as the truck began to bounce over the rough road north. "More of a suburbs girl."

He smiled, which made him look more handsome than usual. He wore faded jeans, a long-sleeved blue shirt and a battered Stetson. She knew if she looked at his feet she would see dark brown boots caked with mud or heaven knew what else.

Abby turned away and looked out the window at the rolling prairie. Here and there she saw a cow and calf, a weathered windmill, miles of fence line. He told her that his great-grandfather bought the place from a homesteader, how his grandmother was married on the front lawn of the house, that his uncle ran away to the army. And Abby listened, watched his face, pretended last night's kiss hadn't happened. Pretended she hadn't felt scalded by an emotion she had no intention of feeling ever again.

He told her a cousin competed in rodeos. He explained why he experimented with a breed of Scottish cattle. He pointed out crop rotation and hay and corn, the distant Rocky Mountains and, closer to them, Blue Nose Creek.

And Abby listened and worried that she liked the man too much. Liked the land too much. Liked the job too much, too. Cowboys were so easy to please. Hot meals and applesauce muffins were appreciated all out of proportion.

Jed stopped the truck when they reached the creek. "I brought fishing gear," he said.

"And I brought lunch," she admitted, though he would have known what she deposited in the truck bed before they drove away.

"We can do both," he answered. So Abby hopped out of the truck and grabbed an old baseball cap she'd found in a closet. The sun was ferocious this time of day, despite the ever-present breeze that forced her to pull her hair back into a low ponytail.

He took the picnic basket from her and their hands touched. She would have sworn the electric feeling reached her elbow before she released the handle.

"You know, I'm not sorry," he said, his eyes dark under the shadow of his hat brim. "About last night. I lied. I'd do it again with half a chance and I don't even know why I'm warning you."

"Neither do I."

He looked at her lips, but he didn't move forward. "Probably wasn't a good idea for us to be alone today."

She shook her head. "No. A terrible idea."

Jed took a step closer. "I guess we're old enough to know better."

"Definitely old enough," she agreed, her sneakered feet planted firmly on the rough, yellowed grassland. Jed removed his hat and dropped it—and the basket—on the ground. She knew she shouldn't smile, but she couldn't help it. "I guess you don't want anything getting in your way?"

He lifted her chin with a gentle hand. "No, ma'am."

"I thought you said this wasn't a good idea."

Jed leaned down and brushed his lips against her in a teasing caress. "As long as we keep both feet on the ground we should be safe."

"Hmm" was all she could manage to say. Abby's arms circled his waist as he found her mouth once again. The man knew how to kiss, was her one and only thought before her brains evaporated into the bright Wyoming sunshine. His lips were firm and warm, coaxing hers to part. Abby clung to him, fingers hooked in his leather belt, while his tongue did lovely things to her mouth and his large work-roughened hands slipped under her T-shirt. His fingers caressed her bare back in slow, easy motions, as if the man had all the time in the world, was one of Abby's crazy thoughts.

She wished it didn't feel so damn good to be kissed and touched and— "Jed," she whispered, pulling away from his mouth a fraction of an inch. "We can't do this."

"Hell, I know," he muttered, refastening her bra with awkward motions. "This is crazy."

She didn't let go of his belt. Her knees were shaking and she didn't want to embarrass herself by falling into the creek. "Maybe we should fish."

"Or eat," he said, removing his hands from her back and pulling down her shirt. He held her shoulders and kissed her neck. His warm breath tickled her ear and made her forget about food and fishing.

"You said we'd be okay if we stayed on our feet," she whispered, wishing she was on her back. Shameful thought, but an appealing one.

"I was wrong. We could do it standing up without much trouble."

Abby took a deep breath. "We can't 'do it' at

all, Jed. A fling with a cowboy isn't in my plans for the summer."

"Neither was working on a ranch."

She bent and picked up the basket. "Would you like lunch now?"

Jed nodded. "Yeah, I guess I would." He motioned toward the grass. "After you."

"I think we should eat in the truck."

She couldn't tell if he smiled or winced. "Lady, sitting in the truck doesn't mean we're going to stay away from each other."

"Yes, it does. There's a gearshift in between the seats. You stay on your side and I'll stay on mine."

"Yes, ma'am." He picked up his hat and dusted it off before putting it back on his head. "And don't worry about a thing, Mrs. Andrews. A cowboy never makes love with his hat on."

9

"I DON'T THINK it worked." Ty took the BB gun away from Matt and watched Jed's pickup lurch across the yard. "And I think she broke the truck."

Trish shrugged and tightened her grip on the baby in her arms. "He won't care what she breaks. He's got it bad."

"You don't know that for sure," he said, pocketing the ammunition.

"Oh, yes, I do." She shaded her eyes with her free hand. "He's teaching her to drive?"

"Yeah. Started yesterday. She can't shift."

"Well, it's tricky to learn something new at Abby's age," she admitted as the truck whined to a stop by the chicken coop. "At least she didn't hit anything."

"She might have ruined the clutch."

"I told you, Ty. Your uncle won't care."

Matt tugged on Ty's arm. "Can I show Mom the gun?"

"Yeah, sure." The kid sure loved that old BB gun. Hard to believe Matt was eight years old and had never shot a can on a fence before. "We'll tell her what a good eye you have."

"That's good, right?"

"Sure is."

Cass tugged on his other hand. "When can I shoot?"

"When you're seven," he said. "When your arms are big enough."

She flexed to show him her muscle.

"Nope," Ty said. "Not yet."

Trish took the little girl's hand. "Let's go see if your mom had fun this afternoon. I wonder how many cows she saw, don't you?"

"Mama," Chrissie said, lifting her head from Trish's shoulder.

"Yep. Your mama's back. Isn't that nice?"

Ty grinned at his girl. "Now will you let me show you the house? I have something you should see."

She giggled. "Oh, yeah?"

"I mean the carpet," he said, feeling his face grow hot.

Trish laughed and kissed his cheek before taking the girls to see Abby, who had opened the driver's door and hopped out onto the dirt. She was smiling. That was a good sign. He waited to see how Uncle Jed looked, but his hat shaded his face. Ty couldn't tell if he was happy or not. Hey, a guy could only do so much and then it was up to Jed. He'd be crazy to pass up a chance to have his very own wife in his very own bed on his very own ranch.

With that in mind, Ty followed Trish over to the truck. It was time to show her what color he'd painted the bedroom.

* * *

"HALLELUJAH!" Bull's face creased into a happy grin. "Just what I've been dreamin' of, Miz Abby. A fried chicken dinner."

"Oven-fried chicken," Abby explained. "Less cholesterol."

"Aw, we don't worry about such things around here," Bull said. "There's a lot of old cowboys around these parts and we've all chewed up our share of beef. Those doctors are good at settin' bones, but they don't know much about what's good to eat." He reached for a hot biscuit, and Cass passed him the jar of grape jelly.

"Where's Jed?" Ty asked, helping himself to mashed potatoes.

Bull shrugged. "Ain't seen him for two days, 'cept for yesterday mornin'."

Abby joined them at the table. "I think he went up to someplace called the 'summer pasture.' Didn't he tell you that, Ty?" Thank goodness. They'd spent the rest of Sunday avoiding each other, and had managed to do the same thing Monday, too. Two middle-aged people who hadn't had sex in a while—well, at least in her case—needed to stay away from each other as much as possible. And that was for the best, Abby decided. She didn't need to be tempted again.

Toby looked surprised. "He went up the mountain?"

"Mom, what chicken is this?" Matt pointed to the chicken platter. No one said anything, but everyone stopped chewing.

"It's just chicken, Matt. Don't worry," Abby assured him. The child glared at the men seated around the table.

"Who killed one of my chickens?"

The three men shook their heads. "Not me," Toby said, "though I've offered to help your mama with that, I admit. Hens get old and that's what happens, son."

"Not to *my* chickens," the boy said, turning to Abby. "Did you kill one of them, Mom?"

"Absolutely not."

"Did Mr. Jed?"

"No."

His lower lip quivered. "Cross your heart?"

Abby crossed her heart and leaned over to whisper, "Don't tell anyone, but I bought the chicken at the supermarket."

"You did?" His face brightened and he leaned forward and helped himself to a drumstick. "Cool."

Abby picked up her fork. "Go ahead and eat, everyone. No one has ever seen these chickens until tonight."

Much later, when she was finally alone, Abby wished every problem could be as easy to solve as buying store-bought poultry parts. Trish and Ty, for example. Late Sunday afternoon she'd seen those two teenagers disappear for over an hour, and she had a good idea what they were up to. She wondered if marriage might be the right thing after all, since they appeared to be so much in love. Better to marry now than to wait until middle age, when love was coated in doubt and maybe even a touch of bitterness?

Abby sighed and kept scrubbing dishes. Tonight she'd waited until after the children were settled in bed to clean up the kitchen. It was easier this way. It was also easier with Jed missing. The man made her think of long, dark nights and warm skin and kisses that touched her heart.

She wasn't meant for one-night stands. She'd never even experienced one. And this summer, in Wyoming, was the wrong time to start. She would have to be strong from now on. No more late-night drinks in the kitchen, no more driving lessons, no more picnics where it was more tempting to be horizontal than vertical. She was thirty-four years old and she needed to start acting her age.

JED FELT SORRY for himself for three nights and two days. He talked to his horse and wished he'd learned to play the harmonica. A few plaintive songs were just what he needed to hear as he sat up there on the mountain shivering in the cold night air and feeling lonelier than a calf who'd lost his mama.

Abby Andrews was one fine woman. She could cook and clean, and she looked damn good pretty much all the time. Even at three in the morning, with her hair all messy, she'd looked like a woman who needed to be loved. Trouble was, he wasn't volunteering to do the loving. Oh, the physical part, sure. He was more than prepared for that, he knew, shifting in his bedroll. But he sure as hell wasn't prepared to take on the raising of three kids. And maybe more, since Abby seemed like the kind of woman who would want more children.

Well, he wouldn't mind a kid of his own, he supposed, staring up into the starlit sky. If he was younger, that is. He was too old to learn how to be a husband, too set in his ways to be a father. And besides, he'd raised Ty since the boy was eight. He'd done his share and now the boy had grown into a man. A young man who was itching to get on with his own life and live with his own woman.

Jed rolled over onto his side and tried to get comfortable. He could be in his own bed right now, instead of baby-sitting a bunch of cows that didn't need baby-sitting. But he didn't want to be in his own bed. He wanted to be in Abby's. He wanted that apple-scented hair tickling his neck, he wanted to bury himself in her tempting little body.

He wanted her to leave. Before he made a fool of himself.

THE CHECK was for three thousand dollars, made out to Abigail Andrews and signed by J.T. Monroe. It was left on the kitchen counter and discovered by Ty, who picked it up and studied it in the dim light of dawn.

Good thing he'd gotten home late, Ty figured. He'd heard all about the Cadillac that Abby had her eye on. She'd asked Bull what he thought a couple of nights ago and they'd had some long conversation about how to buy a used car. Ty hadn't listened. It was Trish's dad's night to play poker, which meant the old man wouldn't be home until dawn.

And Ty couldn't leave Trish all alone out there on the ranch. Not when she was afraid of the dark like she was. So he'd been in a hurry to leave right after supper, but he remembered the three-thousand-dollar price of the car.

Meaning Jed was ready to send her packing. Meaning Jed wasn't any closer to falling in love or having his own life or anything else. And time was running out.

"Mornin'," his uncle said, stepping into the dimly lit kitchen. "What are you doing up so early?"

"Oh, I couldn't sleep," Ty said. Which was true.

Jed yawned and peered at the clock. "It's four-thirty, kid. I guess you're looking forward to a full day's work."

"Yeah, sure." He wanted to crawl into bed and sleep for ten hours, but he'd been caught. "I was just gonna make the coffee."

"You might want to put that check back where you found it, too," Jed drawled.

"Coward," he said, looking his uncle right in the eye.

Jed stopped yawning. "What?"

"I said you're a coward. Anyone can see that

Abby really likes you," he insisted, hoping Jed would believe the lie. "And now you're trying to get rid of her? I'd say that's pretty low."

Jed straightened and took one step forward. "The last man who called me a coward ended up with three of his teeth on the floor at Murphy's. You sure you want to continue this conversation?"

Ty gulped. "I didn't know you were scared of women, that's all."

"Scared of women?" Jed lowered his voice after looking behind him to make sure Abby wasn't there. "I don't think that's ever been a problem."

"Well, prove it, then." Ty took a deep breath and took the folded check from his shirt pocket and handed it to his uncle.

Jed didn't take it, though he looked at it long enough. "She's a real nice woman, Uncle Jed. If you like her why don't you just tell her?"

Jed took the check. "That's none of your business, son."

"How many chances are you gonna get? How often does a nice woman like Abby end up here on the Gem?"

His uncle smiled. "I'd say, not very often."

Progress, Ty figured. Jed agreed with him. Finally. "Well, Uncle Jed, either you want the woman or you don't."

"Does this conversation have anything to do with you wanting to get married?"

Ty tried not to grin as Jed tucked the check in his shirt pocket. "Yes, sir. I know I don't get my mom's money till I'm twenty-five, but I can't wait that long." He wondered if he should tell Jed about the baby. No, he didn't want anyone saying he and Trish *had* to get married. And there was no telling what old man Jensen would do if he found out.

"I'll give it some thought," Jed replied. "Make the coffee while I finish getting dressed."

"And then we'll talk?" Visions of his wedding night flashed through his head.

"No," said Jed, turning away. "Then we'll figure out when we're going to start haying."

"Sure. No problem." Ty figured he'd better quit while he was ahead.

"YOU'RE BACK," was all Abby said in that soft voice that made his chest hurt. "And you made the coffee."

"Ty did," he managed. "He was out late again last night."

She poured herself a cup of coffee, but didn't sit at the table with him. Jed watched her as she took eggs and bacon from the refrigerator and set them on the counter beside the stove.

"I can wait for breakfast," Jed told her, hoping she'd sit with him for a few minutes. He wanted to prove he wasn't a coward, even if Ty wasn't here to witness it. "There's no hurry."

"It's six already. I guess I didn't hear the alarm go off."

She looked tired. And beautiful. "Did Cass have another bad dream last night?"

"No. Chrissie was restless, though. I think she's getting another tooth." She sat at the table and pushed her hair back from her cheek. "I moved her playpen upstairs Sunday night so she wouldn't become too accustomed to sleeping with me."

"She can have her own room upstairs, you know. If that will help you sleep better."

"I might do that, especially since Ty is having trouble with the water faucets at the foreman's house. He said he has to get new parts in town." She took a sip of coffee. "I think that place is jinxed."

"Sure seems that way," Jed agreed, but he wondered if his nephew was up to something more than just repairs. "Maybe I'll have to take a look at the place myself." He knew he should. After all, he'd promised her a place of her own. And it shouldn't matter that he liked the thought of seeing her in the middle of the night.

"Oh, don't do that. He's working hard, really. He's such a nice young man," she insisted.

Jed made no comment. Ty was a good kid, but he liked getting his own way. "Has the Jensen girl been around?"

"She's been helping me with the kids in the afternoons, when her father doesn't need her. I don't think she has much of a home life."

"Well, that's probably true. I wish she and Ty weren't—"

"Weren't what?"

"Never mind." He leaned back in his chair. "Do you like it here, Abby?"

"On the ranch?"

He nodded.

"Yes, I do. Oh, I didn't expect to when I first took the job, but I'm getting used to cooking for so many people now. And everyone has been so good to the children."

"And Spokane?"

"Can wait. I called my mother this weekend to tell her I had a job in Wyoming for a while. She wasn't too happy with the idea, but then again, she wasn't too happy about my divorce, either."

"The divorce was your idea?"

"No, not at first. But when a man wants to leave, does a woman really want to force him to stay?" A look of sadness crossed her face. "I wished things had been different, but now I don't know. I think we're all better off without him."

Jed's heart lifted to his throat and stuck there while Abby rose to make breakfast. He wasn't a coward, he told himself. He just couldn't decide if he wanted to fall in love or not. And he wondered if he had the choice.

SHE CRIED for three nights. Abby walked the upstairs hall and attempted to soothe the toddler whose swollen gums made her scream in pain. Abby dosed Chrissie with liquid Tylenol, rubbed her gums with numbing antiseptic cream and held her until Abby thought her arms would fall right off her shoulders. The first night Jed came upstairs, took one look at the baby's puffy eyes and Abby's pale face and returned with an ornate oak rocking chair. Abby sank into it gratefully and rocked until she was dizzy and Chrissie was asleep.

The second night Jed brought bowls of ice cream into her room. He told Abby he remembered Ty wanting ice cream after he'd had his wisdom teeth pulled out. They took turns spooning it into Chrissie's eager mouth until the child leaned against Abby's chest and fell asleep.

The third night Chrissie screamed in the rocking chair, refused the ice cream and made her mother cry along with her. Until Jed lifted the baby out of her mother's weary arms and into his own.

"Go to bed," he told Abby. "Chrissie and I can walk for a while downstairs."

"I can't—"

"Sure you can," he whispered. "She's going to wake the others if she keeps this up, and you look like you're going to tip over."

Abby couldn't stop the tears that leaked out of the side of her eyes. "I feel so badly for her. Her little gums are so puffy and sore."

"Maybe she'll cut those teeth tomorrow," he said, looking for all the world as if he held babies every night. Chrissie's sobs turned to little shuddering breaths and her chubby arms curled around Jed's neck. "Go to bed," he urged. "I'll bring her back to bed after she's fallen asleep."

"But Ty—"

"Is out with Trish. It's Saturday night, remember? And tomorrow's your day off. You can sleep late in the morning."

It was an offer she couldn't refuse. "You don't mind?"

"Honey, we *all* need to get some rest, so you take your turn now."

Honey? Abby was too tired to protest the endearment. She wasn't even sure she heard him correctly. "Thank you," she told him. "I'll bake you a pie tomorrow."

Jed chuckled and Chrissie complained with a scowl on her face. "Go to bed, Abby," he repeated. "Now."

She did as she was told, climbing self-consciously into her bed as Jed left the room with her daughter in his arms. She heard his footsteps on the stairs, listened to Chrissie's cries and Jed's low voice until the sounds faded and sleep came.

When she woke, Chrissie was asleep in the playpen at the foot of the bed and the house was silent once again. Abby tiptoed out of the room to the bathroom and then down the stairs to the kitchen. She wanted a glass of milk and a handful of sugar cookies; she wanted an aspirin for the dull headache above her eyes. She wanted to sit in a quiet room all by herself and not hear anyone else breathing.

And he was there, of course, leaning against the counter and sipping whiskey from a heavy glass.

"You're supposed to be asleep," was all he said.

"So are you." She decided not to open the refrigerator and stand in the light since she hadn't worn a robe. She peered at the clock. Three already. "You've been awake all this time?"

"We fell asleep in the recliner," Jed admitted. "I just brought her up a few minutes ago. I guess we woke you."

"No." She moved past him and got a glass and filled it with water. Then she found the bottle of aspirin in the cupboard and took two. "I never heard a thing."

"Did you sleep?"

"Like a dead woman." How odd that they had avoided each other for so many days, only to spend the nights together with a fussy baby. And now the baby was asleep and here they stood in a dark kitchen. Jed wore a white T-shirt and jeans, and he was barefoot. She had nothing on but an ankle-length cotton nightgown and a pair of underwear. She had never worn underwear to bed until this summer, when she never knew if there would be a cowboy in the kitchen in the middle of the night.

It was foolish to worry about underwear when she had other things to worry about before dawn, such as getting to Spokane and earning money and finding a place to live before school started and if moving close to her mother was the right thing to do. But when Jed put his hand out and touched her cheek, she stopped worrying. Abby met his gaze and waited, because he looked as if he wanted to say something.

"Apple."

"What?" she whispered as his fingers traced a line along her jaw and to her lips.

"That's what kind of pie I want. Apple."

She told herself she didn't want to be held, didn't need to be loved. Shouldn't lean against him as if without him she would fall to the floor. But he felt so good, so warm and solid, as his arms wrapped around her in an embrace that was at once comforting and passionate. He rubbed her back, his fingers moving in lazy circles across her shoulders and spine.

"Abby." He spoke against her hair. "Come to bed with me now."

Oh, she wanted to. God knows she wanted to feel like a woman again, someone other than a mother and a cook and all those other roles she enjoyed by day. She wanted to strip off his clothes and hers. She wanted to feel hot and naked and unable to breath with the wonder of it all. "I can't," she said.

Silence. And those large hands stilled against her back. "No? Are you sure?"

Abby pulled back enough to look into his face. "No, I'm not sure. I'm not sure of anything this summer. That's the problem."

He smiled and kissed her mouth. "There's no problem," he insisted after he'd kissed her long enough to drive her doubts away. It had been so long—too long—since she'd wanted a man inside her, since she'd needed to make love with that mindless heated joy she could barely remember.

Abby wanted to remember. When Jed lifted her into his arms, she didn't protest. She wrapped her arms around his neck and tasted a soft spot of skin below his ear. When he carried her into his bedroom and laid her inside the sheets on his bed, Abby felt only the certainty that what they were doing was right. Right for the moment, and that was all that mattered.

Abby reached for him and smiled as he tossed his T-shirt to the floor. "I thought you just wanted pie."

"And this, too." His hands skimmed her legs and lifted the hem of her nightgown higher, over her head, to be thrown across the mattress. "I'm greedy."

She reached for the waistband of his jeans and lowered the zipper. "Me, too."

He winced and withdrew from the bed. "If you touch me like that again, sweetheart, this will be over long before either one of us wants it to be."

She heard the rest of his clothing drop to the floor, and then he returned to the bed. He lay on his side and propped his head up on one hand. "I've never brought a woman to my bed before. It's a good thing my nephew left condoms in the bathroom."

Relieved, Abby turned to face him, moving her leg to brush against his. "I never slept with anyone but my husband."

"So there's a first time for everything." He reached out and touched one finger to the tip of her breast, sending a little shock through her body as he teased her nipple for long seconds. "Should I go slow?"

Her body was slick and ready for him. "No. Not this time. Later," she gasped as he helped her wriggle out of her underwear. "I don't think I can—"

Jed hesitated, his big body leaning over hers, his warmth heating her already hot skin. "Don't think you can *what?*"

"Wait," she breathed, welcoming him between her thighs.

"Then we won't," he rasped, fitting himself into her with a smooth, slow motion. She sighed and wrapped her legs around him to bring him closer.

"This is better than baking," she whispered before his lips found hers and his body began to move in a rhythm calculated to bring them pleasure. She heard him chuckle against her mouth, then the exquisite sensation of having him inside of her overtook every thought. He drew the climax from her, a shattering of feeling that spiraled from deep within. He thrust deeper then, finding his own release within moments, his own movements prolonging her pleasure.

After long moments Abby thought she could breathe again. Jed murmured something into her neck. "What?" she asked, not knowing what he'd said. Her fingers found his hair as he lifted his head and looked into her eyes.

"Forget the pie," he said.

She was still laughing when he began to make love to her again.

10

ABBY WAS GONE. Jed, his eyes still closed against the daylight, stretched his arm across the bed and encountered no warm, naked woman beside him. He heard no soft breathing, didn't touch satin skin. He listened for the sounds from the kitchen, but couldn't tell if he actually heard anything or if it was just wishful thinking. He would give a lot for a cup of coffee right now.

Then again, he hoped Abby was upstairs. And asleep. He hoped her kids had left her alone this morning. He certainly hadn't left her alone last night. Jed opened his eyes and contemplated the pleasures a willing woman could bestow. And his body reacted hard and fast to the memories. Last night had been a night like no other he'd ever experienced, and he couldn't really figure out why. Not that he was thinking all that clearly this morning.

Was it because Abby had been in his own bed? He'd never made love to a woman here on the ranch before, not for years, not since Catherine. And that had been in the barn and not the house. Nor did he remember anything like what he'd experienced with Abby. She'd been generous and passionate. She'd enjoyed herself, he'd seen to that, but he felt as if she'd done the giving and he'd done the taking, and Abby had enjoyed it as much as he had.

Damn. What had he done? Well, he thought, tossing the sheet off his body as he sat on the edge of the mattress, what he'd done was made love to Abby. And he wanted to do it again. After all, she was a beautiful woman, and he was only human. They were both adults, old enough to know what they were doing, long past the age of consent. They both knew she was only here for the summer, that there would be no promises made and no future contemplated.

Unless both of them wanted it, of course. Jed ran his fingers through his rumpled hair and winced. If Abby wanted hearts and flowers, a wedding ring and a couple of babies, she was looking at the wrong man. He'd been alone a long time and he intended to stay that way.

Jed stood and headed for the shower. When had life become so complicated?

"THEY DID IT."

"You're kidding."

Ty held the phone closer to his lips. "Nope. I'm sure it happened last night, because I saw Abby going upstairs to bed this morning."

Trish giggled. "Are you sure they really, um, slept together?"

"She came out of Jed's room. What do *you* think they were doing all night?"

"All night?"

"Well." Ty reconsidered. His uncle wasn't exactly a young man, but then again he figured Jed hadn't had sex in a long time. "Maybe not *all* night."

"I hope you're right. Well, it's about time. They aren't getting any younger."

"I'm surprised old Jed could remember how."

"Ty!" She giggled again.

"Well, it's true. He's been whistling all morning, which is a good sign." Whistling ran in the family, Ty figured. He'd been whistling a lot lately himself, and he knew his own reasons. Hell, it wouldn't take a brain surgeon to figure out why Uncle Jed sounded so happy. The man had finally gotten some.

"Now what?" Trish asked. "This means they're in love."

"Yeah," he agreed, though he wasn't so sure. He knew darn well that going to bed with a woman didn't mean you were in love with her, but this wasn't something to share with his future bride.

"You were so smart to bring her home with you, Ty. I can't believe it."

Ty grinned. Yeah, he was pretty smart, all right. "This is progress, honey. I'm going to see if he stays in a good mood before I talk to him about us. If I can get past the part where he tells me that I'm too young to get married, I think I can get him to listen to reason."

"Okay. Want me to come over?"

"Can you?"

"I can try. Dad said he's going out with his friends, but I don't know when. I'll tell him I'm baby-sitting, which wouldn't really be a lie. Abby might need help with the kids this afternoon."

"Good idea. You don't mind?"

"I love her kids, you know that. And I think I need practice with diapers and high chairs and everything. And Abby said she'll teach me how to make pie crust whenever I want."

"I've got to go now," he said as Jed walked past him and over to the coffeepot. He whistled an old Willie Nelson tune and poured himself a cup of coffee. "Maybe you can stay for supper."

"I'll try. I love you."

"Yeah," Ty whispered. Abby, the baby on her hip, entered the kitchen. "Hurry up."

"I will. 'Bye."

Ty hung up the telephone and hoped like hell that today was going to be a good day. He wondered if Jed and Abby would start acting like they were married. Or if they would pretend they hadn't been together in that way. Maybe older people weren't as impressed with sex as younger people. Maybe it wasn't so important that anyone that age acted like it was big deal.

"Good morning," he heard his uncle say. And Abby answered, just the way she always did.

"Good morning, everyone," she said. "I see someone made the coffee already."

"Yeah," Jed said. "It's not too old, either."

"Oh, good."

All of a sudden Ty wasn't sure if he wanted to

be in the same room with the two of them. He didn't want to picture them naked. And he didn't want to picture anything more than that, that was certain. He closed his eyes for a minute and opened them when he heard his name being called.

"Ty? You okay?" Jed sat down at the table. "Come sit and we'll go over the day."

Ty turned around and didn't move. "I thought we were supposed to be doctoring calves."

"Yeah," Jed said. "But you'd better take Bull with you instead. I've got work to do around here."

"I can stay here and clean the barn if you want."

"No." He motioned to the chair across from him. "Get some coffee and sit down."

"Do you want breakfast, Ty?" Abby asked, settling Chrissie in the high chair.

"No, ma'am, I ate already."

She blushed. "I slept through the alarm. Chrissie had a bad night and kept me awake a lot."

Abby started mixing cereal for the baby, Ty concentrated on keeping Chrissie from chewing on his fingers, and all of a sudden Jed looked real busy studying his coffee mug, the one with the geyser on it that he'd bought when they visited Yellowstone six years ago.

Ty figured he'd better say something before the two older people had heart attacks. "Has she gotten her tooth yet?"

Abby smiled. "She sure did. This morning I felt

the tiniest little point popping up, so maybe she'll start feeling better. And sleeping more."

Chrissie reached for Ty, who he leaned sideways so the baby could pull on the fabric of his sleeves. "Hey, Chris. How's it goin'?"

Jed took a sip of coffee. "She sure seems happier than she was last night."

"Yes. Your eggs will be ready in a minute."

"This is your day off, Abby."

She looked surprised but she didn't stop fixing oatmeal. "I forgot. And besides, you have to eat. Both of you."

Jed rose and walked over to the counter. "Go back to bed. Ty and I will give Chris her breakfast and then we'll bring her upstairs."

"You will?"

"Sure."

If Ty had had any doubts about what happened last night, he sure didn't have them anymore. If Uncle Jed was offering to baby-sit, he must feel pretty damn good this morning.

"Well, maybe I will," Abby said. "Her oatmeal needs to cook for another minute and then you add milk and let it cool down."

"No problem." Jed touched her shoulder and turned her toward the door. "Go get some rest."

Ty knew he shouldn't stare, but he couldn't help himself. He watched Jed's fingers curl over Abby's shoulder for the slightest moment, as if she was his woman now. Possessive, even. He didn't know Uncle Jed could be that way. "Don't worry, Abby," Ty said, after clearing his throat.

"Trish will be over soon and we'll take the kids for a ride."

Maybe that would give Jed and Abby more time to be alone. No telling what might happen, Ty figured. By evening Jed would be in such a good mood he'd agree to anything, even a wedding.

IT WASN'T AS IF she had to marry the man, for heaven's sake. Great sex, for a few brief and wonderful hours, did not equal a commitment. Besides, Abby thought, removing her sandals and crawling into her own bed, she knew better than to expect commitments from anyone. She could only depend on herself from now on—and hadn't she learned that the hard way?

But another thing she'd learned was that if you had a chance to rest, you took it. Even if you had already showered and made the bed, you could lie carefully on top of the bedspread and close your eyes and count backward from fifty and never make it to twenty-five.

And when you'd spent half the night making love to a cowboy, you didn't make it past forty-two.

"MAYBE WE SHOULD TALK about my future," Ty said, pouring himself a fresh cup of coffee.

"Ba, ba, ba!" the baby hollered, smashing oatmeal against the tray of the high chair. She grinned at Jed. "Ba, ba?"

"Heck, no. That's oatmeal and you're making a

mess," he said, turning to Ty. "What do I do with her now?"

"Clean her up."

"Well, get me something to clean her up *with*." He eyed the child splattered with oatmeal. Somehow he'd managed to feed her, but right now it looked like most of her breakfast coated those chubby little fingers. Ty handed him a wet dishrag and Jed went to work cleaning up the protesting baby. She squawked a little when he wiped her nose and mouth, but otherwise tolerated it. Jed had to rinse out the cloth three times before the baby was no longer sticky.

Ty placed some plastic toys on the tray. "We were gonna talk about my future."

"We were?"

"Yeah. I've been cleaning up the foreman's house, and—"

"Don't," Jed said. He didn't want Abby to move, not now. That bunkhouse was too far away, and besides, it wasn't in good enough shape for her. Not even after Ty killed the rats and fixed the plumbing.

"Huh?"

"Don't spend your time on that anymore," he ordered. "There's too much wrong with that place."

"Uh, Jed, I don't—"

"Forget it, Ty. Abby's staying here in the main house. I don't want her or the kids getting hurt. And it's better that, ah, she's close to the kitchen." He bent to pick up the bright yellow duck toy and handed it to the baby, who squealed with glee and tossed it onto the floor again. "What should I do with her now?"

"She's fine. She just likes to throw things. Trish said that all kids that age throw their toys down, so people will pick them up. It's a game." Ty leaned forward. "I really need to talk to you, because—"

"Where's Mommy?" Cass asked, looking around the kitchen as she walked into the room.

"Sleeping," Jed explained. "She was tired so she went back to bed for a nap."

Cass frowned at him. "Is she sick?"

"Nope." The child's expression didn't change, so clearly there was more explanation needed. "Your sister cried a lot last night, so your mom didn't get much rest."

Cass nodded. "Chrissie can really scream loud when she feels like it."

"She outdid herself last night." He was surprised when the little girl climbed up in his lap. Jed looked at Ty for help, but his nephew only shrugged as if to say *she's all yours*, so Jed pushed his coffee away from the edge of the table and wondered how he'd gotten himself into this in the first place.

"This is all your fault," he told his nephew. Ty didn't grin, the way he usually would. "Hey, I was kidding."

"Yeah." Ty stood and shoved his hat on his head. "I guess this isn't going to be a good time to talk to you."

"That's right." Cass snuggled against his chest and yawned. "And if you're going to start in about getting married, you might as well save your breath."

"You don't understand. There's something—"

"I understand more than you think I do," Jed interjected. "And I don't want to see you getting in over your head. You'll be twenty-five soon enough, and that's when you can make all the decisions you want."

"I'm not waiting six more years," he said, with a glance toward the kids. "I'm ready to make a life for myself."

"You're too young," Jed repeated, wondering what happened if oatmeal got stuck in the baby's ears. "And that's final."

"No, it's not." Ty walked out, slamming the door behind him.

"I'm hungry," Cass said, lifting her head and staring at him with those gray eyes that looked just like her mother's. "May I have toast, please?"

"Sure." He lifted her onto the chair beside him and went over to the counter. He could fix toast, he could doctor calves, he could sell beef at a good price and he could even make love to Abby Andrews twice in one short night. But he sure as hell couldn't figure out what was going on with his nephew, except that the boy was in too much of a hurry to grow up.

Meanwhile, all he could do was hope the sun set early tonight. He wondered if Abby would be beside him when it did.

* * *

ABBY DIDN'T KNOW what to do with herself, but she knew she wasn't going to cook today. The thermometer on the side of the porch showed the temperature to be ninety-two, the ever-present wind blew dust every which way, and the house was empty. Her children had disappeared, along with everyone else. Abby had taken another shower, braided her damp hair in a loose knot at the base of her neck, and put on her prettiest sundress. She wandered through the rooms of the large house, she straightened newspapers and spotted a magazine Ty had been searching for. She had no desire to go to town, to drive the hour to Carson and run errands. Besides, it was Sunday. A day of rest. A day to recover from Saturday night.

But she wouldn't think about Saturday night. Or early Sunday morning. She wouldn't think about Jed's long, lean body and rough, warm skin. She wouldn't think about how good it felt to have a man inside her. To have a man's arms hold her.

No, she wouldn't think of that. She poured herself a cup of cold coffee and dropped ice cubes into it, then looked out the windows for signs of children and cowboys. For the first time in years she felt at peace. And not because of the sex, though that had been something wonderful. No, today she was rested and alone, in a place she had grown to like very much. Nothing was permanent—she'd learned that the hard way these past years—but this Wyoming ranch was the closest she'd come to a solid life-style.

Her children, wherever they were this morning, would be safe. These rough Wyoming men would see that they were. Trish would make Ty blush with the desire to touch her, Jed would pretend not to notice, and the other men would do their jobs and enjoy their dinners and behave as though Abby's presence here was something that would last. But she wasn't going to stay. Everyone knew that she was only here for the summer.

"Abby?"

She turned to see Jed enter the kitchen. "I didn't know anyone was here."

"I was cleaning up," he explained, running his hands through his damp hair. "I thought maybe you'd want to go to town later on."

"Why?"

He shrugged. "I could take you out to eat. There's a place in town that serves a pretty decent Sunday dinner, and Trish and Ty offered to baby-sit the kids."

"I'd like that." She told herself she shouldn't be shy. She was thirty-four, and she'd spent seven hours naked with this man. "Where is everybody?"

"In the barn. Trish is letting the baby pet a calf."

He sat down beside her and glanced at her cup. "Cold coffee?"

"Help yourself."

"I'll pass."

They sat in silence, while Abby wondered what she should say to a man on the morning after.

He cleared his throat. "When do you want to go?"

"Any time. Maybe after the kids go down for a nap?"

"What time is that?"

"Around one."

He smiled, the slow easy smile of a man satisfied with life. "What are we going to do with ourselves between now and then?"

Lovely threads of passion spun between them, and Abby couldn't do anything but answer his smile. "I could bake that pie."

"To hell with the pie." He took her hand and brought it to her lips. "Do you still taste like me?"

"You could find out," she managed to say. "If you think we have the time."

"We could do it fast now, and slow tonight," he suggested, putting her palm to his lips.

She would have had sex with him on the table if she wasn't thinking clearly. "That tickles."

"That's not what a man wants to hear, sweetheart."

"What exactly *does* a man want to hear?"

"The word *yes* will do just fine."

She smiled. "You keep seducing me in the kitchen, did you know that?"

"Honey," he drawled, pushing his chair away from the table, "I'd seduce you in every room in this house if you'd give me half a chance."

"The bedroom will be fine, Mr. Monroe." She

glanced out the window and saw no sign of any-one. "But we'd better hurry before anyone comes inside for lunch."

"Yes, ma'am." He tugged her toward the hall. "I think I can accommodate you just fine."

Abby couldn't help laughing. It was delicious to be wanted. She hadn't felt so lighthearted since the days before she became engaged. This wasn't love, of course, she reminded herself, hurrying to keep up with Jed's long, determined strides.

This was better than love.

"I lied," he told her, after they'd removed their clothes and tossed them on the floor.

"About what?" Abby was too busy leading him to the bed to really care about the answer to her question. Making love in the afternoon was a luxury not to be wasted. Didn't the man realize that?

"I'm not going to hurry," he said, following her down to the mattress. His body covered hers, set-tling between her legs in a tempting motion. Abby wriggled against him as he pinned her wrists above her head with one large hand.

"You're not?" She smiled and he nuzzled her neck.

"Nope. I like seeing you in the daylight too much to go fast." He dipped his head lower, to her breast, while his free hand ran along the smooth skin of her thighs. Jed released Abby's hands and slid lower, his tongue teasing her ab-domen and then lower. He held her thighs apart with his big hands as his mouth found her, made her tremble, sent heat radiating through her languorous body. She was powerless to control the climax caused by his tongue and his lips. It burst inside of her, against his mouth, with an unexpected jolt of pleasure. And while her body still trembled with delicate aftershocks, Jed entered her. She liked being slick and ready for him. He covered her body with his own and made love to her again, and this time neither one of them thought about the time.

"DO YOU THINK we've been doing this long enough?"

"No," Trish replied. "We're going to give them time alone. As much as we possibly can."

"Jeez, how much time do they need?"

"Ty!" Trish shook her head, as if telling him not to talk about it in front of the children, but Ty felt restless and edgy. He was starting to wonder if this had been such a good idea after all. Jed was having sex while *he* was baby-sitting kids. How had that happened?

"Is there any more?" Cass asked, holding out her hand. Ty gave Cass another handful of chicken feed and let her shake the grain inside the pen. Matt came out of the henhouse with a bucket of fresh eggs.

"Look," he said, "I've got sixteen today!"

"Cool."

Trish set the baby on her feet and held on to her hands so she could walk over to her brother. "No,

Chrissie, you can't touch the chickens. They might peck at your fingers."

"I think we could go in now," Ty moaned. "Weren't we going to paint the living room today?"

"We're baby-sitting," Trish reminded him. As if he didn't know. "And anyway, I can't be around paint fumes," she said. "The chemicals aren't good for the baby."

Cass turned around to look at her. "What baby? Do you have a baby, too?"

Ty froze. "There's no baby," he answered for Trish. "Just Chrissie."

The little girl frowned at him as if she knew he was lying to her, then stared at Trish's stomach. "Do you have a baby in there?"

"Uh, no," Trish said. "But maybe someday I will. If I'm lucky like your mommy."

"I know how babies are made," the little girl announced. "Do you?"

Ty choked back a laugh and looked at Trish. "Do you know how, Trish?"

"Maybe." She smiled down at Cass and changed the subject. "You're a very smart girl. I'll bet you know all sorts of really neat things. Do you know how to blow bubbles with bubble gum?"

Cass shook her head. "I'm not allowed. Mommy says it will stick in my hair and make a mess."

"Yeah," her brother said. "Mom had to put

peanut butter in her hair to get the gum out! It was gross!" He wrinkled his nose.

Trish laughed. "Next time I'm in town I'll buy gum and teach you and Matt how to blow bubbles," she promised. "But I'll ask your mom first if it's okay."

"Neat!"

Matt tugged on Ty's arm. "Can I shoot the BB gun today?"

"Sure." He sighed, resigned to taking care of kids instead of sneaking off with Trish. He took Trish's hand and squeezed it. "You want to take the girls back to the house?"

She shook her head. "I think we'll go to the other house instead and play there."

"Play what?" Cass asked.

"Play house, of course." Trish took her hand and led her toward the foreman's house. "I really like to do that." She grinned at Ty, who suddenly didn't want to shoot the BB gun at all.

"Come on," Matt said, heading toward the barn. "I don't want to play with the girls anymore."

"You'll change your mind when you get older," Ty said, sighing. "One of these days that'll be all you think about."

"Yuk," the boy said. "I'd rather eat dirt."

"Yeah, well, that's what you think now," Ty said, throwing his arm around the boy's thin shoulders. "But you might have a point there, kid. I guess some days it's easier to eat dirt than know what to do about women."

"Yeah," the boy agreed. "Girls are a pain. Except my mom. She's okay."

"I like those cookies she makes," Ty agreed.

"She lets me help." He shot Ty a worried look. "It's okay if cowboys know how to cook, isn't it?"

"Heck, kid, it's a matter of survival. Men hafta know how to do that stuff, and a cowboy who can make cookies is worth his weight in gold."

"Really?"

"Would I lie to you?"

Matt hesitated. "I don't want a *cooking* nickname. I want something really, really tough."

Ty watched Trish walk away with the girls. He wanted something, too, but it had nothing to do with BB guns and nicknames. He wanted to get married. He didn't know why such a simple thing had gotten so darn complicated.

11

HE COULDN'T BELIEVE he was out on a date. Of course, Sunday dinner at Chuck's Steakhouse wasn't exactly Denver's Brown Palace, but Abby didn't seem to mind. He wondered if women got tired of their own cooking after a few years, but he couldn't imagine Abby getting tired of applesauce muffins or oven-fried chicken. No one could.

"Why are you smiling?" Abby set her oversize menu on the table and gazed at him with an expression that made him want to take her back to the ranch. Back to bed.

"I was thinking about your fried chicken," he said. She looked a little worried. If he hadn't known better, he'd have sworn she looked guilty.

"Is there something wrong with the chicken?"

"Of course not," he hurried to say. "I was just thinking of all that pot roast we ate before you came."

"Oh." She looked relieved. "I thought you might have had some complaints...or something."

What man in his right mind would complain about anything that Abby Andrews did? "I didn't mean—"

The waitress interrupted them to ask what they wanted for dinner, so Jed felt as if he was off the hook. He hadn't been on a date for so long that he'd forgotten how to act. He sat there across the table from Abby and kept thinking of making love to her a couple of hours ago. He was the luckiest man in Carson, that was certain. And if he continued to act like this, he'd be worse off than his lovesick nephew. Clearly he had to get hold of the reins and get himself under control.

"It was nice of Trish and Ty to baby-sit for me today."

"Yeah, well, I keep thinking they must be up to something."

"Like what?"

"Who knows?" He shrugged. "They want to get married, but I won't go along with that idea, and I'll bet Trish's father wouldn't approve, either."

"Then why don't they elope?"

He frowned. "They could, I supposed, 'cept I hope I raised the kid better than that. And Ty doesn't inherit his father's share of the ranch until he's twenty-five. Until he does, he sure as hell can't support a family. Besides, Trish's father isn't about to let her go anywhere."

"She seems very mature for eighteen."

"Without a mother, the girl's had to grow up fast, I guess."

The waitress brought Abby's wine and Jed's glass of beer and set them in front of them.

"Thanks," he said, then lifted his glass to

Abby's. And then he couldn't think of anything to say.

"To young love," Abby whispered. "And baby-sitters."

"Yeah," he said, touching his glass to hers. "A man could get used to this."

"To what exactly?" she asked, her eyes twinkling as she smiled at him.

"To having you on the Gem," he replied, wishing he didn't want to lean across the table and kiss her. If he did, the folks in Carson would talk about it for two years.

"That is a lovely thing to say."

Hell, after last night and this afternoon, he was just about exploding with "lovely things" to say.

Maybe Ty had been right. Having a woman around wasn't half bad.

"LIFT UP SLOWLY," Jed cautioned, and Abby did as he told her as she eased her foot off the clutch. "Now step on the gas more."

"I think I'm getting the hang of this," she said as the car moved forward without lurching.

"Yeah," the man beside her said. "You're doing just fine."

"Thanks." She managed to flash him a quick smile before turning her attention back to the dirt road that connected the outbuildings. "I'd really like to be able to go to town without someone having to drive me all the time."

"I told you, I don't mind."

"But you have your own work to do, and so do

I." And just because they made love at night didn't mean she shouldn't—or wouldn't—do her job during the day. Although, she thought wryly, she did tend to take more naps with the children in the afternoons this past week. And now it was Saturday again, and she was determined to travel to town on her own.

He chuckled. "Trying to get away from me already?"

"No, but if I don't get groceries you won't have much to eat next week." She guided the car as it bounced down the driveway. She didn't want to get away from him at all, and that was the trouble. She liked it here. She liked it too much.

"Well, drop me off here at the horse barn, then. I can keep Matt with me this afternoon, if you want."

She pulled up in front of the barn and put the car in neutral. "He'd like that. He's not much of a shopper and Trish could only stay for a couple of hours this morning." She glanced at her watch. "She's probably wondering where I am."

Jed touched her cheek before he opened the door and got out of the car. He shut the door and leaned into the open window. "You be careful, honey, and don't be too anxious to get into fourth gear."

"I won't." She left him, then, driving back to the house to get the girls. She'd promised Trish a ride home, she had a list of groceries, and she wanted to get a new nightgown.

Don't be too anxious to get into fourth gear, Jed

had said. Good advice. The Gem had begun to feel like home. And Abby knew all too well that homes came and went. She and the kids would go on their way at the end of the summer. There was no sense rushing into feelings she knew wouldn't last.

Besides, Abby thought, shifting into second gear as smoothly as if she'd been doing it for years, even if she was in love with Jed, there was no reason to do anything but keep it to herself.

"Uncle Jed," Ty called, getting out of his truck. He'd been trying to find Jed all day, ever since he'd missed him at breakfast this morning. They'd all been busy with the haying for days. Too many days, in Ty's opinion. He was running out of time.

Jed waved and disappeared into the house. He was never late for supper anymore. Since his Sunday "date" with Abby, Jed had been on time for supper for five straight days in a row. Between the food, the kids and the cook, Ty hadn't been able to get his uncle's attention for more than fifteen seconds at a time. He slammed the door of the truck and started brushing dirt off his clothes. Damn it all, he was going to have to figure out a way to get Jed alone. Long enough to explain a few things, anyway, and then he'd just have to hope for the best.

Ty entered the kitchen and sniffed. "Hey, everyone," he said. He ruffled Matt's hair and sat beside him. "Fried chicken, huh?"

Abby smiled and put a platter of chicken in the middle of the table. "Shouldn't you wash up first, Ty?"

Damn. He pushed back his chair. "Yes, ma'am," he said, his stomach growling. When he returned, everyone's plate was piled high with chicken, mashed potatoes and carrots. Including his.

"I fixed you a plate," Abby explained. "Toby, would you pass the rolls to Ty?"

"Why, sure, Miz Abby," the old man replied. "I think there are a few of 'em left for the kid."

"Thought you had a date tonight," Jed drawled.

"Thanks, Toby." He took the basket and emptied it of three rolls. "Why'd you think that?"

"It's Friday."

Matt nodded. "You and Trish go to the movies on Friday."

"That so?"

"Yup."

Ty took a big bite of chicken and chewed for half a minute. "Guess you have me all figured out."

"Are you gonna get married?"

"Yeah, eventually." He glanced over at Jed, who was busy taking a spoon away from the baby and didn't seem as if he'd heard. "Or I'm gonna be in great big trouble."

"Trouble?" the child echoed, while Toby and Bull laughed. There were enough jokes made after that to let Ty have three helpings of chicken and eat uninterrupted.

Ty waited until supper was over, then he followed his uncle into the living room. "Uh, Jed—"

"Come here, Ty," he said. "I need help with this kid."

Chrissie hung on to Jed's large thumbs and tried to walk toward Matt, who hurried to protect his *Star Wars* action figures from the approach of his baby sister. "Don't bring her over here, Mr. Jed! She likes to chew on the heads."

Ty sighed and went over to the baby, who grinned at him and drooled. "What do you want me to do?"

"Watch her for a few minutes while I see if Abby needs any help."

"Yeah, sure," Ty said, swinging the baby into his arms. He sighed as Jed left the room. He and Trish had wanted Jed to get a life of his own, to know what it was like to be in love. Now Jed was hanging out in the kitchen instead of in the barn.

Well, hell. They'd created a monster.

Jed didn't know what was the matter with him. He was forty years old. Too old to be hanging on to babies. Too old to admire a little girl's crayon drawings, or to be teaching another fatherless boy how to be a ranch hand.

"I've got work to do before dark," he said more gruffly than he intended.

Abby looked up from scrubbing a pot. "Well, go do it, then."

"But the kids—"

"Will be fine," she said, grabbing a towel and drying her hands. "I can finish this later," she assured him in a soft voice, though she didn't look at him when she said it.

"Ma-ma," Chrissie called, unwrapping her arms from around Jed's neck. She wriggled against him. "M-m-m-ma?"

Jed set her on her feet and held on to her hands. "Think she's ever going to walk on her own?"

"Sure she will. She's just a little more cautious than Matt and Cass were." Abby dropped to her knees and held out her arms. "Come to Mommy, honey."

Chrissie clung to his fingers and wouldn't let go, so Jed walked her over to her mother. "I don't think she's feeling real brave right now." And he knew exactly how the little girl felt. He took a few steps backward and remembered why he wanted to leave the house.

"No, I guess not." Abby tried to take the child into her arms, but Chrissie would have none of it. She turned toward Jed and giggled.

"Okay, kid," Jed said, sitting on his haunches and waiting. "Come on over."

The baby began a wobbly walk toward him. She never noticed that her mother released her hands, that she walked the last two feet all by herself, but her mother did.

"She walked!" Abby cried. "I can't believe she walked over to you!"

Jed caught the baby around the waist. "Yeah, she sure did."

"She walked to you," Abby said. "That's amazing."

He pointed the baby toward her mother. "Why?"

"She doesn't know you that well." Abby held out her arms. "Come here, sweetie."

Jed grinned. "You talking to me or to her?"

"To her. I thought you had work to do."

Jed released Chrissie's waist and the baby stood on her own, but she didn't move. "Yeah, well, it can wait."

"Come on," Abby urged her daughter. "Come to Mommy." Chrissie began a hesitant walk, then wobbled faster as she tumbled into her mother's waiting arms. "Good girl!"

"Why are you crying?"

"Because this means she's growing up," Abby sniffed. "She won't be a baby much longer."

She looked like a baby to Jed. She looked like a baby who had his heart in her fist. Just as her mother did.

Jed stood and grabbed his hat from the hook by the door. "I've gotta go." He hesitated as he watched Abby hug her daughter. "I could see if one of the men would baby-sit, if you wanted to go into town and see a movie."

She shook her head. "Thanks, but I don't think Toby and Bull are ready for diapers and bottles."

"Yeah, I guess you're right." And Ty was in the shower getting ready to go out with the only other baby-sitter within fifteen miles. "Guess you're stuck here."

She smiled. "I don't feel stuck. Do you?"

No. He didn't feel stuck. He was in love. Pathetically and dismally in love. "I'd better go," he replied, backing out of the kitchen. If he didn't leave soon, he might say something he'd regret. Abby didn't intend to stay in Carson, she sure as hell didn't intend to be a ranch cook for the rest of her life. She wouldn't consider staying, he was sure. Not even if he asked. Which he wasn't going to do.

No, he decided, his long strides taking him across the yard toward the corrals. He wasn't going to make a fool of himself. He wasn't going to rush into anything. Hadn't he been giving Ty the same advice?

"COME ON, Cass. Let's go see if we can find the calves." Abby and the girls fed the chickens, then took a short walk around the corral. The ground was too uneven for Chrissie to attempt to walk, so Abby carried her on her hip. Matt had gone off with Ty in the truck, and Trish was coming over for a while so Abby could go to town. It was time she started shopping for a car, maybe took that Cadillac out for a test drive if it was still for sale. It was long past time she got rid of the van. Not that she was going anywhere, but it was the middle of July already, and there were decisions to be made. She couldn't stay here on the Gem forever, no matter how much she wanted to.

And no matter how many weeks she'd been sleeping with the boss. The old foreman's house was still empty. Jed hadn't mentioned her moving into it again, but if she stayed—and if this affair of theirs came to an end—moving to the little house might be a solution. It could be a solution anyway, because Abby knew she was too much in love to be living close to Jed Monroe and keep her feelings hidden.

The blue door was unlocked. Abby stepped inside and saw a tiny kitchen that had been recently painted white. The smell of paint still hung in the air and in the room just beyond the kitchen, a roll of blue carpet lay in the corner. Someone had been stripping the old linoleum from the floor, revealing a large corner of plywood underneath.

"It's like a playhouse, Mommy," Cass said, peering up the stairs while Chrissie wriggled to get down to walk on the wood floor of what Abby supposed was the living room.

"Yes, it is," Abby said, helping the baby to balance herself. Had Jed been working on it for her? Somehow she doubted it. Ty was the one who spent time here, and the disastrous place he'd described didn't mesh with reality. Chrissie plopped down on the floor and clapped her hands.

"Mommy?"

"Where are you?"

"Up here!"

Abby picked up Chrissie and went up the narrow staircase. "Cass, be careful. You don't know what's—" She stopped in the hallway, in view of the two rooms that were clearly meant to be bedrooms. One held a double bed, complete with mattress, pillows and blankets, as if someone was sleeping here already. This room had been freshly painted, also, but there were no curtains at the window or rugs on the wood floor. Abby opened the closet door and saw that it was empty. Whoever belonged here had yet to move in. She peeked into a tiny bathroom, then went into the hall to find her daughter.

Cass stood in the other room and held up a teddy bear. "Mommy, this is the kid's room."

An understatement, Abby realized, noting the parts of a crib stacked against the wall. Someone was going to be putting it together. And that was usually the father's job.

The father. Abby went to the tiny four-paned window that overlooked the west pastures. Someone around here was planning on having a baby. Someone was fixing up the house for a family, and she knew darn well that this renovation hadn't begun the day Jed ordered Ty to fix it.

"Put the teddy bear back where you found it," she told Cass. "It isn't right to touch things that don't belong to us."

"Where's the baby?"

Chrissie giggled. "We're not talking about you," Abby laughed. She looked down at Cass. "Where's the baby?" she repeated. "Well, I don't know." But she had a sneaking suspicion everyone was going to find out pretty darn soon.

"Maybe Mr. Jed knows."

"I don't think we should talk to Mr. Jed about

this. I think this should be a secret, Cassie." She held her daughter's gaze with her own. "Do you understand?"

Cassie's eyes lit up. "I *love* secrets, Mommy."

"Me, too," Abby answered. Sometimes. "Let's think of this as a 'secret house,' and not tell anyone that we've been here, okay?"

"Okay." Cass solemnly waved her little hand over her chest. "Cross my heart."

"Good." She had to think about this, though she had a feeling she'd seen all the pieces of a puzzle. Putting this together wasn't going to require an extra amount of IQ points. "Come on, ladies. I think we'd better get back to the house. It's nap time."

"I'm not tired."

Neither was Abby, but she wanted some time alone. "I'll read you a story first."

"Can I sleep in your room, with Cass?"

"Sure. If you're quiet."

"I'm *always* quiet," the little girl said, following her mother down the stairs. "Matt's the one that makes all the noise."

Abby hurried out of the little house and hoped that no one had seen them. She wouldn't want either Jed or Ty thinking she'd been snooping around. Which she had been. But just in the context of examining a place that Jed said she could live in, of course. Ty had gone to a lot of trouble to keep the place's renovation a secret, but Abby had the feeling that his secrets couldn't be kept much longer.

That crib was in that little room for a reason. She didn't know why she hadn't realized it before now.

"TALK TO ME a minute?" Abby set a glass of iced tea in front of the teenager and then sat across the kitchen table.

"Sure, Abby." Trish looked at her watch. "And then I'd better get home. Dad will be expecting his supper at six."

"Are you close to your dad?"

Trish shrugged. "Not really. He's not around much."

"Oh." So how was she going to bring up the subject of having babies? And why did she think this was going to be easy? "Ty says that you two are planning on getting married someday."

The pretty teenager smiled. "We have a lot of plans."

Abby took a sip of iced tea. "Want to talk about them?"

"What do you mean?"

"Woman to woman. Talk. About anything."

Silence. Trish looked down at her hands, and when she finally met Abby's gaze her cheeks were flushed with embarrassment. "You know, don't you?"

"I saw the house. And the crib."

"I told him he shouldn't have put that in there so soon. It was Ty's. He found it in one of the sheds." She reached for a napkin and wiped her eyes. "We didn't want anyone to know."

"People are going to know eventually, Trish. Something like this can't be hidden for long." Except sometimes, Abby remembered, thinking of things she'd heard on the news. Teenagers sometimes hid their pregnancies for nine months. "How far along are you?"

"About three months, I think."

"You think? What does the doctor say?"

Trish reached for another napkin. "I haven't seen a doctor yet."

"Honey, you have to." Abby took a deep breath and hoped that she wasn't going to sound too bossy. "It's really important when you're pregnant. You have to see a doctor as soon as possible, to make sure the baby is going to be okay."

"He'd tell my father, and my dad would kill me."

"How old are you?"

"Eighteen."

"I don't think he'd have to tell your father, Trish."

"He would anyway. Daddy and Doc Adams play poker together every Friday night."

"Then you're going to have to tell your father. And Ty is going to have to tell his uncle."

"He's been trying, Abby." The girl wiped away another waterfall of tears. "Mr. Monroe is just too busy with—" She stopped and bit her lip.

"With me," Abby finished for her.

She nodded. "We thought it would be good for Mr. Monroe to fall in love. So he'd know what it was like for *us*. We thought then he'd understand and he'd let Ty have his share of the ranch early."

"That was quite a plan."

Trish blew her nose. "It didn't really work out, Abby. At least, not yet. We didn't think he'd get so, uh, happy that he'd forget Ty was around."

It was Abby's turn to blush. "You think he's happy?"

"Sure he is. But he still won't listen to Ty when he wants to talk about getting married."

"Maybe Ty should start talking about having a baby instead." She handed Trish another napkin. "Ty has to start taking responsibility for this, and you have to start seeing a doctor."

Trish sniffed. "Yes, ma'am."

Abby got up and hugged the girl's shoulders. "Don't worry, honey. This will all work out just fine."

"That's what Ty always says, too."

Abby hoped they were both right, but she didn't want to be in the room when Ty told his uncle that there was another Monroe on the way.

12

FATHERHOOD wasn't going to be easy. Hell, Ty thought, he couldn't even manage to get married, never mind become a father. A legal one. Well, all that was going to change. He was going to do what he should have done six weeks ago, when Trish had told him that the pregnancy test she'd bought at the drugstore had turned out positive.

Abby's spiced meatloaf would be his last supper as a single man. "Could I have the potatoes, Bull?"

"Sure, kid. What are you in such a hurry about?"

"Nothing." He knew he had to keep up his strength. He'd be driving most of the night before reaching the Nevada border.

"Tell us a story," Matt begged the old cowboy. "Tell us the one about your nickname again."

"You've heard it three times," Toby mumbled.

"Yeah, but I'm trying to figure out how it works."

Abby wiped the baby's face with a cloth. "How what works, honey?"

"'Honey' is not a nickname," Matt declared, and Ty quit listening. He hoped the baby was a boy. His son would be born a Monroe, no matter what happened. The house was ready and that baby would be born in January, to Mr. and Mrs. Ty Monroe. After tonight no one would be able to say they were too young to get married.

"I really need one," Matt whined.

"Ty, quit your daydreamin' and pass the green beans over here, son."

He looked to see Toby laughing at him, so he pushed the bowl of beans toward that end of the table. "Yeah, sure."

"I'll bet Ty has a date," Matt said. "It's Friday."

"I sure do, kid," he replied, and pushed back his chair. "And if I don't hurry and clean up, I'm going to be late." If he didn't get busy and pack the truck, they wouldn't get on the road in good time.

"Have a good time," Abby said when he passed her chair.

"And try to get home before dawn," Jed added.

Ty didn't answer. By dawn everyone would know he wasn't coming home **all** by himself.

ABBY WAS GOING TO TELL him about the pregnancy. No, she wasn't. This was none of her business, she reminded herself. And yet there was a baby coming, and none of these people seemed to understand that Trish needed to see a doctor.

She was going to tell Jed when he came in from the barn tonight. As Ty's uncle, he needed to know. She'd waited three days to hear from Trish, three days for Ty to talk to Jed, three days for Jed to discuss this with her. Abby cleaned up the kitchen in record time, took a bath while the children watched television for thirty minutes, gave all of them ice cream and hustled them into bed by eight o'clock. She would find out what Jed knew, and then she would feel better.

She was going to tell Jed, of course she was. Abby hadn't expected him to surprise her in the living room and kiss her until she couldn't breathe for wanting him. She didn't expect to be pulled into the shower with him, couldn't resist washing the most intriguing parts of his body with soapy hands, loved the feel of all that slick male skin against hers. If it had been a tub and not a shower stall, they would have made love right then and there, he'd said.

And she'd dared him to do it anyway. After that it had taken her a while to remember what she had wanted to talk about, but as they lay together in his bed Abby remembered that she needed to talk about Ty.

"Jed," she murmured, lifting her head from his shoulder. "There's something I think you should know."

He frowned. "Sounds ominous. Are you leaving the ranch?"

"No. I mean, not yet."

He continued to frown, but he smoothed his palm across her cheek. "Why are you looking so worried, darlin'?"

"Someone has to tell you and I guess that someone is me."

"Tell me what?" He ignored the faint sound of the telephone ringing.

"Don't you want to answer that?"

He almost smiled. "Honey, I'm in bed with a beautiful woman. Do I look like I want to answer the phone?"

She glanced downward. No, Jed was ready for something, but it wasn't conversation. "No, I guess not, but—"

"Do we have to talk?" He leaned over and kissed the tip of her breast.

"Yes. Just for a minute." A very fast minute, she decided, her thoughts jumbling as Jed's lips teased the sensitive skin of her breast. "It's the baby," she gasped. "You need to know about the baby, and decide—"

"What?" He lifted his head and jumped back a little.

"What you're going to do about it," she finished, a little sorry that she'd started this subject. Damn Ty. He should have been the one to do this. "Didn't Ty tell you?"

"Ty knows?"

"Yes, and it's fine with him. He's very happy."

Jed stared down at her. "He's very happy," he repeated. "What the hell does Ty have to do with this?"

Abby sat up and reached for the sheet. Once it was wrapped around her she turned back to Jed. "Because Ty—" she began, and then stopped. Jed was in the process of getting out of bed and reaching for his clothes. "What are you doing?"

He stopped buttoning his shirt, but he wouldn't look at her. "Damned if I know."

And that's when she knew. She'd seen that stunned, trapped expression before, when she'd told Greg she was pregnant with Chrissie. He hadn't wanted either of them, and he'd managed to make that clear when he'd gotten dressed, packed his clothes and walked out. "It's too bad you don't have a suitcase," she said, sliding out of the bed. She found her robe and put it on, fastening the belt tightly around her waist.

"What?"

"Never mind." So he thought she was having his baby. "How the hell could this have happened? I've made sure I used a condom every time."

"Nothing's perfect," she said, watching him tug on his boots. She was glad she sounded so calm and unemotional when she could easily have skinned him with a paring knife.

"Jed!" Bull's voice roared through the locked bedroom door. "Open up!"

Jed unlocked the door and positioned himself so that Bull couldn't see Abby. "What?"

"The hospital—Trish just called," the old man panted. "Jeez, Jed, Ty's been shot. Jensen caught them running away."

Abby hurried to the door. "What?"

The men ignored her. "Where is he?"

"Carson Hospital."

Jed threw the door open. "He's alive." It was a statement, not a question. And Abby held her breath for the answer as she followed the men down the hall.

"Yeah. Trish said he was still hollering when the ambulance came."

"You coming?" Jed asked, and Abby opened her mouth to say yes when she realized he had been talking to Bull.

"Hell, yes," the old man said. "Toby's brought the truck around and he's waiting for us."

Jed was halfway through the kitchen before he turned to Abby. His tormented expression tore at her heart.

"Call me," she said. She couldn't come with him, not with the children sleeping upstairs.

"Yeah." His gaze dropped to her abdomen and then back to her face. "Yeah," he repeated, grabbing his hat and turning away. Abby waited until she heard the sound of the truck engine disappearing down the road before she poured herself a drink.

She prayed for Ty and swore at Jed and waited in the kitchen for the phone to ring again. Men were all alike, whether they wore those damn cowboy hats or not.

TRISH WOULDN'T STOP crying, not when the sheriff tried to question her about why her father had shot her boyfriend. Or when whiskey-soaked Jensen tried to explain, before the deputies arrested him, that he'd caught the kids eloping and was only trying to scare that cocky little bastard. Or when that really young-looking doctor came into the waiting room and told them that Ty was going to be okay. A shoulder wound, the young man told them. Out of the hospital in a day or two, would need physical therapy to get the use of that arm back.

"Can we see him?"

The doctor shook his head. "He's not back in his room yet. As soon as he starts to come to, I'll have someone get you."

Trish thanked the doctor and kept on crying. Jed tried everything to get her to stop. He sat beside her on the orange vinyl couch in the hospital waiting room. He gave her his handkerchief, he held her hand, he even had Bull find a nurse to help out.

"My fault," she gasped, wiping her eyes for the fiftieth time. He didn't know why she bothered, but now that he knew Ty was going to be okay he could concentrate on the little filly. He wished he could send the boys for Abby. A woman would come in handy right now, even if he hadn't reacted real well to the news that the woman was pregnant. One problem at a time, he told himself. He'd fix that one when he got back to the ranch. He hadn't had much time to figure out what he was going to do about being a father, but that queasy feeling in his gut wouldn't go away.

A matronly nurse approached them. "The doctor ordered a tranquilizer for you, honey," she said to Trish. "Maybe you should think about taking it before you wear yourself out."

Trish took a shaky breath. "I can't." She

blushed and turned away from Jed. "I don't want to take anything to hurt the baby."

"The baby," Jed repeated, dread laying thick and heavy on his heart. "What baby?"

The nurse nodded. "I'll check with Dr. Mack about that. I'll be right back."

"What baby?" Jed asked again.

"Mine and Ty's." The tears started dripping again, but Jed was out of patience. He was damn well going to know what was going on around here and he was going to know *now.*

"Trish, stop crying for two minutes and tell me what happened tonight," he ordered in his best "boss" voice. It seemed to work, thank goodness. She wiped her eyes and took another deep breath before answering.

"We were going to Nevada to get married. The baby's due in January and we didn't want to wait any longer. I'm starting to show." She looked at his blank expression. "I'm starting to look pregnant," she explained. "We didn't want anyone to know we *had* to get married."

"I think people would have figured it out."

"By then it wouldn't matter," Trish said, sniffing. "And then Abby told me that I should see a doctor soon and that Ty should tell you about the baby right away."

"Then why the he—heck didn't he?" The baby Abby had been trying to tell him about was Ty's baby, not his? God, he felt like such a fool. Such a disappointed fool.

"He tried, Mr. Monroe. He said you wouldn't

listen. First you said he was too young and then after Abby and you, well, you know, you didn't want to talk about anything."

"Jed?" Bull handed him a cup of coffee. "We went to the cafeteria and got some coffee to keep us goin'. Trish, I got you some tea, just like you asked. Least I think that's what you said, cuz I couldn't rightly tell."

"Thank you," she said as Bull set the cup on top of a stack of magazines on the table beside her. "Tea's great."

The nurse returned with a cup of water and a pill. "Here, honey, you take this and get yourself calmed down. Your young man is going to be just fine."

Jed set his coffee aside and waited for Bull and Toby to sit across from him in the small waiting room. "Did you call Abby?"

The men looked at each other before answering. "Yep," Toby said, cradling his coffee cup between his hands as he leaned forward. "Told her the boy was gonna be just fine, told her that old man Jensen—" Toby stopped, darting a glance at Trish. "Well, anyway, I called her. She was real happy to hear Ty was okay."

Jed looked at his watch. Past midnight already, too late to call her himself. She'd probably gone to bed after hearing the news. "Why don't you two take Trish home and go home yourself? Get some rest."

The two ranch hands shook their heads and Trish started weeping again.

"We'll take care of you, Trish," Jed insisted. "I didn't mean go back to your father's house. Go back to the ranch and crawl into Ty's bed." And he bet it wouldn't be the first time.

"What about you, boss?"

"I'm staying here." He wouldn't rest until he saw for himself that the boy was going to be all right. "You can come get me in the morning."

By morning Ty would be awake, Trish would have dried up, and things would start getting back to normal.

IT WOULD NEVER be the same. Abby knew she might as well face that fact sooner or later. Oh, she made the coffee and baked a couple of batches of applesauce muffins. She fried eggs for the men before they left for hospital, and she buttered toast and made small talk with Trish. She made sure the kids were dressed and clean and watching Saturday morning cartoons without arguing. But, despite pouring coffee and rinsing dishes and listening to Trish, Abby was thinking. Thinking a lot.

"Trish, do you want to tell me what happened last night?" she said, unable to contain her curiosity any longer.

"Daddy'd had too much too drink," Trish explained. She lowered her voice so the children wouldn't hear. "He wouldn't have shot Ty otherwise. We were getting ready to leave when he came home from the poker game early. He *never* comes home early from poker."

Abby poured herself a cup of coffee and sat at the table. "Bull said you were eloping to Las Vegas?"

Trish shrugged. "Somewhere in Nevada, I guess. Anywhere we could get married real fast."

"And then you were coming home and moving into that house out there and living happily ever after."

Completely missing the sarcasm, Trish smiled and sipped her tea. "Ty's fixed it up real nice, hasn't he?"

Abby sighed. "Yes, he has."

"Mr. Monroe said that we could get married as soon as Ty is feeling better, but that I had to see a doctor as soon as possible. I told him you said that was real important."

By now even a thickheaded cowboy like Jed would have figured out that the baby she'd been talking about last night wasn't his. Abby wished she'd been there to see his relief about escaping fatherhood and any obligation to the woman he'd hired as a summer cook. She'd have to be careful about showing her feelings, though. There had never been any promises, never any talk of the future. Just because one of them was in love didn't mean that both of them were.

She patted Trish's hand. "Ty will be home before you know it, and then we'll see about getting that wedding planned. I think it's long overdue, don't you?"

Trish smiled through her tears. "I really hope you stay on the ranch, too, Mrs. Andrews."

"Oh, I think I'll be on my way by the end of August," she said. "I'm going to stick to my original plan." Which was not to get involved with men. Not to fall in love. And most of all, not to turn into a cheerful domestic goddess who believed in happy endings.

"YOU HAFTA DO SOMETHING," Bull moaned, following Jed out of the house. "Them biscuits of hers were hard as rocks."

Biscuits weren't the only thing hard around the Gem, Jed knew. Abby had stayed away from his bed for two weeks now, ever since the accident. "What exactly am I supposed to do? Tell her her cooking isn't any good?"

The old man turned pale. "I don't know if you should do *that*, knowin' how sensitive cooks are."

Jed stopped and tipped his hat back. The morning sun was already burning his face, and there were three days of work to fit into two. They were one man short, and the cook wasn't talking to him. "Then what?"

"Fix whatever's wrong, boss. Give her a raise. Or get her some new pans or something. I sure don't mind lumpy potatoes, but burned chicken is harder 'n hell to chew." He lowered his voice and tilted his head toward Jed's. "I think she forgot how to make coffee, too."

"Yeah, I noticed." Yesterday afternoon the local newspaper had been folded to the classified ads, which meant Abby was more interested in shopping for cars than baking cinnamon rolls.

He shoved his hands into his pockets and contemplated the oddness of women. Since Ty had come home from the hospital, Trish had grown from a weeping teenager into a stubborn female determined to repair her man. The wedding had been fast, while the father of the bride was out on bail and available to give the bride away. Since then the two teenagers had been kissing so much Jed figured their lips were going to dry out and blow to Utah.

Ty acted like he was dying half the time, just so Trish would take care of him. It was sickening what marriage did to a man. Then again, Jed wouldn't mind a little bit of that attention for himself. He wondered if he should have one of the men run over him with a tractor, just to see if Abby cared.

Then again, it might turn out to be a waste of good blood.

"Jed, I think you'd better see this," Toby said, sticking his head in the door of the cattle shed.

"What?" He let go of the calf he'd been doctoring for scours and went to the door. He wiped his forehead with the sleeve of his shirt.

"I can't really do it justice. You have to see for yourself."

Jed hid a sigh. His stomach grumbled as he followed Toby to the hog pen. Those peanut butter and jelly sandwiches at lunchtime sure didn't stick to a man. He would have to talk to Abby, have to apologize for thinking the baby was his.

Maybe then she'd start putting baking soda in the muffins and freshly ground coffee beans in the pot. "I don't have time—"

"Yeah, you do." He pointed toward the boar, who lay down in a far corner of the pen. "Take a look at that."

Jed whistled. The boar's testicles had swollen to the size of basketballs. "What the hell happened to him?"

A tremulous voice behind them said, "I did it. And I don't care what you do to me."

Jed turned around. Matt's face was stained with tears and dirt, and he held Ty's old BB gun in his right hand. "Jeez, Matt, what did you do?"

"I shot him in the nuts," the kid announced. Anyone would think he was proud of that fact. "I didn't want to kill him, so I shot him in the nuts instead."

"Why?"

"He ate one of my chickens." Matt's voice began to tremble. "Cass left the gate open and one of 'em got out and followed me to the barn, only she flew into the pen and then that…that mean old hog just ate her." He swallowed hard. "In one bite."

"So you thought you'd kill him?"

"No, sir." The boy's shoulders straightened. "I just wanted to hurt him, you know, in a soft spot."

Toby and Bull turned back to look at the boar, who was obviously not looking for any more hens for lunch.

"Them boars are mean," Toby agreed.

He nodded toward the gun. "I can't have all those BB pellets in the hog pen, Matt. We're going to have to figure out how to get them out before he eats them and gets sick."

"Ty ran out of BBs, Mr. Jed. So I used milo."

Toby nodded. "Smart kid. You may have gotten yourself a nickname after all. Maybe *Wyatt Earp*. We'll have to talk to Bull."

Matt's face brightened. "You think so? Really?"

"Not so fast," Jed said. He leaned down and touched the boy's skinny shoulder. "You can't go around hurting animals, Matt. This old boar will forget about this in another hour or so, so there's no real harm done, which is real lucky for you and for him. Do you understand?"

"Yes, sir."

"You had lunch?"

"Nope."

"Well, your mom will be looking for you, so you get back to the house. But clean yourself up before she sees you. I think this should be just between us men."

"Okay." He held out the gun. "Do you want this back?"

"No, you hang on to it. A good shot like you might just come in handy."

Matt hesitated for a second, then flung his arms around Jed's neck. He held on for a good long time while Jed patted his back and told him that it was going to be okay. When the kid finally released him, Jed handed him a red bandanna. "Use this, son. Take it with you."

Matt, obviously embarrassed by his tears, ran off toward the house while the men watched.

Toby stuck his hands into his pockets and rocked back on his heels. "Looks like you got yourself another boy to raise, Jed."

He surprised himself by liking that idea. In fact, he liked it just fine. "You think I've become a family man, Toby?"

"Nah." The old cowhand chuckled. "I think you've been one all along. You just didn't want to admit it."

Jed thought about that for a long minute. "Guess I'd better go talk to Abby."

Toby brightened. "You gonna ask her to make that special meatloaf tonight?"

"No. I'm going to ask her something more important than that." But first he was going to talk to Trish. And then he was hoping that Wyatt Earp Andrews didn't get his evil ideas for revenge from his mother.

"I'M REALLY BUSY right now," Abby told her boss. *Her boss* was how she had been trying to think of him for the past two weeks and she was beginning to get the hang of it. She looked at the pot of spaghetti sauce and wondered if she'd remembered to add salt.

Jed removed the wooden spoon from her hand and set it on the counter. "Not that busy," he said.

"Very busy." She started to reach for the spoon

but *her boss* took it from her and tossed it in the sink. The back door slammed and Trish bounced in.

"Hi, everybody," she called, going right to the high chair to greet the baby. Matt and Cass were in the middle of a card game at the kitchen table, so Trish smiled at Abby. "Why don't you get out of here for a minute?"

"Thanks." She untied the apron and tossed it over the back of an empty chair. "I could use some air."

"No," Jed said, taking her arm. "You could use some rest."

He led her down the hall and into his bedroom. Abby swung out of his grip and put her hands on her hips. "Just what do you think you're doing? I have sauce to simmer and three kids—"

"That Trish will watch." Jed kicked off his boots and then set his hat on the bureau. When he began to unbutton his shirt, Abby headed for the door. He blocked it. "Nope. We're going to finish our conversation where we left off two weeks ago."

"I think you made yourself clear," Abby said, folding her arms across her chest. "You thought the baby was yours and you sure didn't want anything to do with it."

"You can't take a man by surprise like that, sweetheart." The shirt fell to the floor. "It's not fair."

"No, having children and not wanting them isn't fair." Darn, she wished she wasn't going to cry. Abby blinked. Hard. "But the men I fall—get involved with don't seem to be the fatherly type, so I guess I'm out of luck."

He unzipped his pants. "Not exactly." In a matter of seconds his pants, briefs and socks joined his shirt on the braided rug.

"Having sex with you is out of the question," Abby informed him. "That part of my job is over. And I've got a job cooking at the steak house starting September first."

"You're not leaving town?"

"No," she said, her chin high. "I never really wanted to live in Spokane anyway and I've grown used to Carson. My mother said she'd visit as soon as I found a place to live."

Jed gave her a hurt look, but he didn't say anything as he pulled the covers back on the bed and climbed in. He left a space in the bed for her and lay on his side toward her. "You don't have to get undressed if you don't want to, Abby, but I'd sure appreciate it if you'd tell me again about that baby."

Abby slowly approached the bed and sat down on the edge of the mattress. "You know it's not yours."

"Tell me again anyway."

She took a deep breath and tried to remember her exact words. "I suppose I could have phrased it better," she muttered.

"Well, that's true, but let's not cast blame." He rubbed her back and waited.

She wished it didn't feel so good to be touched.

"I guess I said something like, 'You need to know about the baby.'" Abby turned to look down at him. "And then you jumped up and started talking about birth control."

Jed winced. "Could we back up to the baby part? Say it again."

"You mean, 'You need to know about the baby'?"

He tugged on a lock of her hair so her lips were close to his. "I've always wanted a baby," he said, and he kissed her. "Or two or three."

She shook her head. "Liar."

Jed grinned. "Well, maybe not always. Just since I met you. Are you going to marry me and make babies, Abby?"

"Because you don't want to start eating pot roast again? Because your house is clean and your kitchen counters don't have ants? Because you like my biscuits?" *And not because you love me?* she wanted to scream.

"I love your biscuits, darlin', but I can hire another cook and you can do anything around here that you want."

"What about my kids?"

"They *can't* do anything they want, but they're darn good kids and I like having them around."

"I mean, are you willing to help me raise them?"

He smiled, a smile that made Abby's heart ache with hope. "Yeah. And I'll raise one or two or three more, if you like." Abby pulled her T-shirt over her head and slipped off her shorts.

"I guess you're undressing because you're saying yes?"

"Oh, darn." Abby rehooked her bra. "I can't do this. The kids—"

"Are with Trish."

"But—"

He kissed her shoulder. "I told her—and Ty— that we were not to be disturbed until tomorrow. God knows those teenagers have had more than their share of sex lately, and you and I aren't getting any younger."

"But—"

He eased her under the covers and alongside his naked body. "What's wrong now?"

"Are you sure, Jed? I don't want to make another mistake. I don't want another divorce or another broken heart."

"I've waited forty years to fall in love, Abby. It's not going to go away."

"Are you sure?"

He brushed her hair away from her cheek and looked at her as if she was the most wonderful thing he'd ever seen. "Sweetheart, tell me you love me or get out of this bed."

Was it possible she'd found the right man after all? He offered love. And a home. And he wanted to be there for her kids. *Their* kids. She could bake and clean and order him around for the rest of her life if she wanted to. Abby sighed with contentment and squirmed closer to that big naked body of his. "I love you, you idiot," she said, "and I'm not going anywhere."

A sneak preview of the next
Boots & Booties story

by Kristine Rolofson

THE RIGHT MAN IN MONTANA

Temptation #712

On sale December 1998,
wherever Harlequin books are sold!

1

KAREN BROCKETT surveyed the crowded bulletin board and looked for a spot to place her notice. A spot she could reach. A spot sure to be noticed by the mothers coming in and out of Buttreys. The *perfect* spot. She carefully handed four days of hard work to her little sister. "Don't drop them."

"I won't." Janie gripped the flyers with mittened hands while Karen rearranged the bulletin board and Pete kicked a shopping cart with the toe of his boot. Karen, the eleven-year-old, hesitated over an ad for free kittens—there were two white ones and everybody knew white kittens were the smartest—before moving four business cards off to the side. No one was going to want their carpets cleaned right before Christmas, and besides, their ad was the most important.

Janie shivered as the doors opened and a blast of cold air swept in. Karen glanced toward the two women who walked past them to get shopping carts. *Too old.*

"You sure you're not gonna get in trouble?" the little girl asked.

"I'm sure," Karen replied, and her younger siblings knew better than to argue. "I put the boring stuff over here and made room in the middle. Okay, give me one." Janie obediently held out the flyer.

"Stupid," the little boy mumbled as he kicked at another shopping cart. "It's a stupid idea and you're—"

Karen shot him a warning look. "Don't call names."

"Can if I want to," he said, shoving his hands in his pockets. "Can we go home now?"

"Pretty soon."

"Can we look at the toys?"

"It's a *grocery* store, Pete," Karen said, sharing a thumbtack from the business card of an insurance company with a corner of her blue piece of paper. "Not a toy store."

"They have toys," Janie dared to insist. "Not a whole lot, but some."

"Can I go look?"

"In a minute." She wanted to make sure this was exactly right.

"How many more days?"

"Ten." She didn't have to ask what he meant. He was only five, and it was December. They were running out of time.

Pete sighed. "That's a lot." He frowned up at his big sister. "Are you sure this is gonna work?"

"I hope so." Karen stepped back and studied her work. She'd used the computer at school and made a special heading in bold print. An attention getter, that's for sure. And better than writing it by hand and looking like it was done by a kid.

"Where's Uncle Joe?"

"At the dinner." She'd told her uncle they had Christmas shopping to do, and he'd been too busy talking to the waitress to see his niece tape a piece of blue paper to the window that held all the other important announcements. "We'll go back soon."

Janie stamped her feet. "My toes are cold."

"Okay. Come on." Karen took the remaining two flyers from her sister and then grabbed Pete's bare hand. "Did you lose your mittens again?"

"They're in my pocket."

She led the kids around the store until they found the aisle that had an assortment of baseball cards, action figures and puzzles. "You can look at the toys," she said, "but we're not buying any."

"Santa's coming," Janie said. "Isn't he?"

"Sure he is." If Uncle Joe remembered to send in the catalogue order in time. Karen wished she was four years old again and still believed in Santa Claus. It would be a lot easier than being the eldest and having to be the boss and worrying about everything.

She let the little kids check out the toys for a precious few minutes before tugging them toward the door. The front of the store was crowded with women waiting in the checkout, their carts piled high with food and wrapping paper and other special things that made Christmas so pretty. Maybe she could talk Uncle Joe into coming back here and buying candy canes.

"Did our mommy make cookies?" Janie asked.

"Yes," Karen said, though it was getting harder and harder to remember those years. "Lots and lots. With green sugar and silver candy balls stuck on top."

"Wow."

She stopped before leaving the store, just to see if anyone was reading their ad, but that corner of the entry was empty. Karen blinked at the sudden stinging behind her eyes. She never cried. Never, ever. Crying was for babies and everyone knew that Karen Brockett was all grown up. No one even asked her what she wanted for Christmas anymore. Which was why she had to get it all by herself.

"THE BIGGEST FOOL in all of the universe is sitting right here in a parking lot in Montana," Sylvie Smith told her son. The baby didn't pay a bit of attention. Why would he, when he was busy having a late lunch? She shouldn't be sitting in a rapidly cooling car talking to herself. Anyone who passed by would think she was half-crazy, and maybe they would be right. Especially if the last week was any indication.

She could blame her behavior on postpartum depression. She could say that she talked to herself because that's what single mothers do when there is no one else to listen. She could blame a December trip to Willum, Montana, on a desperate case of foolish optimism. She could explain that she'd hoped for another miracle to follow the miracle of childbirth, but she doubted anyone would understand.

"This is what happens when Mommy gets greedy," she told her son, making sure every inch of him was snug against the cold, tucked inside her worn ski jacket, while he finished nursing. "Or this is what happens when mommies lose their jobs and run out of money."

Oh, not quite out of money. She had enough cash left for a motel room and food, if she was frugal. There was gas money to get back home, but no job and no home when she got there. She'd pinned hopes on finding a new home in Willum, a small town that most people never would have heard of, smack dab in the middle of Montana. And her luck had run out.

"This is what happens," she murmured, shivering a little as the wind whipped around the car, "when mommies believe what daddies tell them."

Sylvie's stomach growled, reminding her that nursing mothers—insane or not—had to keep up their strength. She would buy some groceries and make her way back to that motel she'd spotted on the other side of town. It wouldn't do any good to feel sorry for herself, but then again, it was crystal clear that this wasn't a good week to waste money on lottery tickets.

"Come on, sweet pea," she told the sleeping baby. "Let's go shopping." Sylvie wiped his chin with a tissue, rearranged her clothing and pasted a confident smile on her face before getting out of the car. She huddled over the baby, keeping the blanket over his face, until she was inside the supermarket. Overheated and bright, it was a welcome change from the car. Sylvie bundled little Dillon into a shopping cart and, smelling fresh coffee, decided to treat herself to a cup and five minutes of pretending that life was normal again. The sign in front of the carafe said Help Yourself, so Sylvie did exactly that. She sat down in one of two plastic chairs and, making sure that Dillon was not in a draft, sipped the hot liquid and tried to figure out what she was going to do with the rest of her life.

When that became too depressing, she watched the people who entered the store. There were preoccupied men, women with lists and children, three rowdy teenagers and two elderly ladies who clung together as if holding each other up. The teenagers examined a nearby community bulletin board and then giggled loud enough to wake Dillon.

"Do you see this one? My mom would really think this was funny."

"I need a job, but I don't need a job *that* bad."

"I think it's pretty cool," another said. "Like in a book."

"Jessie, you're an idiot," the tall one added, snapping her gum. "Nobody's *that* desperate. Hey, look! Kittens! Think my mom would let me get one?"

Sylvie stood to comfort Dillon, who went right back to sleep when the girls lost interest in the bulletin board and wandered away. "Good boy," she whispered, readjusting the thick blanket before turning to the bulletin board to see what job advertisement had amused the young people. It was there in the center of the board, neatly typed on a blue piece of paper.

It had to be a joke. Sylvie read the words carefully, waiting for a punch line. No, it seemed serious enough. Concise. Direct. She'd heard of these kinds of things before. There had been a Texas billionaire on *Oprah*, and the man who had rented a billboard. She'd heard people adver-tised. To be fair, she supposed it wasn't much different from putting an ad in the Personals column of the newspaper.

Nobody's that desperate. Wasn't that what one of the teenage girls had said? "Desperate" was sitting in a supermarket in a strange town and being grateful for a free cup of coffee. "Desperate" was wanting your child to have a father and not being able to find him. "Desperate" was talking to yourself in front of a bulletin board. Sylvie leaned closer and read it again.

Woman aged 30–40.

Sylvie pretended to consider whether or not she was qualified for the job. She'd be thirty in a few months.

Cooking and cleaning skills very important.

Which meant he was a practical man who liked his meals hot and his house clean. Yes, she could cook and clean. She'd been doing it since she was twelve.

Must like children.

That was easy, she thought, glancing toward Dillon. Obviously the man who'd placed this ad had a child of his own. And he cared about that child.

Experience preferred, but not necessary.

Sylvie thought of Dillon's father and the months they'd spent together. Did that make her experienced for this job? No comment.

Apply in person at the Rocky T Ranch, 24 miles north of town on Highway 10.

She didn't know where Highway 10 was, but she had a map of Montana out in the car.

She wasn't considering this job, she told herself, dropping the empty paper cup into a nearby garbage can. She hoisted the strap of her handbag over her shoulder and pushed her shopping cart away from the bulletin board's ridiculous plea. She would buy some disposable diapers, peanut butter, bread and milk. Maybe she'd splurge on a couple of oranges if they were cheap enough. Sylvie waited in the lengthy checkout while Dillon, who wanted his diaper changed, screamed loud enough to drown out "Jingle Bells" on the loudspeaker and refused to be consoled.

"The little darlings get tired, don't they," said an elderly woman with a kind smile.

"Yes, they sure do." She tried not to look pathetic.

"He sounds tired. He'll be fine once you get him home and settled in his own bed."

"Yes," was all she could answer before the woman turned back to the cashier to write a check for her groceries. Sylvie rocked Dillon in her arms and waited to pay for her food. Yes, the baby would be better when he was settled in for the night. But Dillon didn't have a home and his bed was a padded playpen she'd bought at a Salvation Army shop. All along she'd thought that Dillon would have a father, only she'd been wrong. She would survive, but her son would be the one to suffer the most.

Sylvie managed to pay for her groceries without dropping the baby or having a nervous breakdown, an accomplishment she promised to herself that she would celebrate later. She made it through the automatic door and into the parking lot before she hesitated. She could return to the car, return to a very uncertain future.

Or not.

It was time, long past time, to be sensible. And practical. Sylvie took a deep breath and trudged back into the supermarket. She'd promised her son a father and she was damn well going to try to get him one. And in time for Christmas, too.

The blue flyer was still there, its bold plea shouting at Sylvie from ten feet away.

HELP WANTED: WIFE

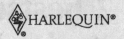

Not The Same Old Story!

   Exciting, glamorous
romance stories that take
readers around the world.

   Sparkling, fresh and ten-
der love stories that
bring you pure romance.

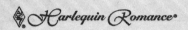   Bold and adventurous—
Temptation is strong women,
bad boys, great sex!

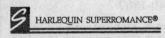   Provocative and realistic
stories that celebrate life
and love.

   Contemporary
fairy tales—where
anything is possible
and where dreams
come true.

   Heart-stopping, suspenseful
adventures that combine the
best of romance and mystery.

   Humorous and romantic stories
that capture the lighter side of
love.

Take 2 bestselling love stories FREE

Plus get a FREE surprise gift!

Special Limited-Time Offer

Mail to Harlequin Reader Service®

3010 Walden Avenue
P.O. Box 1867
Buffalo, N.Y. 14240-1867

YES! Please send me 2 free Harlequin Temptation® novels and my free surprise gift. Then send me 4 brand-new novels every month, which I will receive before they appear in bookstores. Bill me at the low price of $3.12 each plus 25¢ delivery and applicable sales tax, if any.* That's the complete price, and a saving of over 10% off the cover prices—quite a bargain! I understand that accepting the books and gift places me under no obligation ever to buy any books. I can always return a shipment and cancel at any time. Even if I never buy another book from Harlequin, the 2 free books and the surprise gift are mine to keep forever.

142 HEN CH7G

_____
Name   (PLEASE PRINT)

_____
Address   Apt. No.

_____
City   State   Zip

This offer is limited to one order per household and not valid to present Harlequin Temptation® subscribers. *Terms and prices are subject to change without notice. Sales tax applicable in N.Y.

UTEMP-98   ©1990 Harlequin Enterprises Limited

DEBBIE MACOMBER

invites you to the

HEART OF TEXAS

Join Debbie Macomber as she brings you the lives
and loves of the folks in the ranching community
of Promise, Texas.

If you loved Midnight Sons—don't miss
Heart of Texas! A brand-new six-book series
from Debbie Macomber.

Available in February 1998
at your favorite retail store.

Heart of Texas by Debbie Macomber

Lonesome Cowboy	February '98
Texas Two-Step	March '98
Caroline's Child	April '98
Dr. Texas	May '98
Nell's Cowboy	June '98
Lone Star Baby	July '98

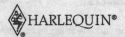

HARLEQUIN®

HPHRT1

Heat up your summer this July with

Summer Lovers

This July, bestselling authors Barbara Delinsky, Elizabeth Lowell and Anne Stuart present three couples with pasts that threaten their future happiness. Can they play with fire without being burned?

FIRST, BEST AND ONLY
by Barbara Delinsky

GRANITE MAN
by Elizabeth Lowell

CHAIN OF LOVE
by Anne Stuart

Available wherever Harlequin and Silhouette books are sold.

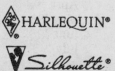

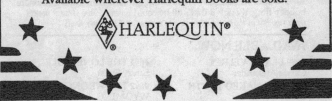

COMING NEXT MONTH

#693 1-800-HERO JoAnn Ross
Hero for Hire

When Lucas Kincaid agreed to guard the *very* delectable body of writer Grace Fairfield, he had no idea what lay in store. Someone wanted the beautiful Grace dead, and the list of suspects was long. But his biggest challenge was making the woman who wrote about happy endings believe that Lucas could be the man for her.

#694 THE PRINCESS AND THE P.I. Donna Sterling

Billionaire heiress Claire Richmond had run away to sow some wild oats, only to realize she wasn't equipped to deal with the "real" world. Luckily, her cousin sent a detective after her. With strong and sexy Tyce Walker by her side, Claire had no fear…which only proved to Tyce what a complete innocent she was, and what a rat *he* was.

#695 SINGLE IN THE SADDLE Vicki Lewis Thompson
Mail Order Men

Daphne Proctor used *Texas Men* magazine to find a husband—and it worked! She was already half in love with cowboy Stony Arnett just through his letters. But nothing had prepared her for the overwhelming chemistry that sizzled between them in person. It seemed like fate. Until Daphne discovered Stony *hadn't* placed the ad—and that he had no use for a wife….

#696 SUMMER HEAT Pamela Burford and Patricia Ryan

Sand and surf, romantic sunsets, a house on the beach…and a sexy stranger to share it all with. What more could you ask from a vacation? In *July*, uptight Quinn could have lived without mellow Molly, who showered naked outside and stayed up all night…. In *August*, Tom wished Sally wanted him for more than just a passionate holiday fling, though if that's all he could have…. *Two steamy novels from two hot authors, together in one very special summer read!*

AVAILABLE NOW:

#689 BLACK VELVET
Carrie Alexander

#690 THE NAKED TRUTH
Dani Sinclair

#691 THE LONE WOLF
Sandy Steen

#692 THE WRONG MAN IN WYOMING
Kristine Rolofson